HANDSOME COWBOY

LORI WILDE
LIZ ALVIN

D1707482

S
he was going to kill her brothers. All three of them. Slowly. In front of the entire town of Honey, Texas.

How dare they invite Jared Kendrick to Trent's wedding? No, not only invite him, but also have him in the wedding party. Were they insane? Was this some kind of lame joke?

Whatever the cause, they were dead men for sure.

"The wedding was beautiful," said Amanda Newman, wife of the minister who'd performed the ceremony. "Trent and Erin seem so happy. Now all your brothers are blissfully married. Guess it won't be long until you follow their example."

Leigh barely resisted the urge to gag. As if. She'd rather go swimming with piranha. She'd finally married off her last meddlesome brother, and from this point on, she'd be an independent woman.

No way was she giving up her freedom anytime in this century.

"I'm too young to get married," she told Amanda. Standing on her tiptoes, she scanned the wedding reception crowd, looking for her brothers.

How hard was it to spot three tall men in tuxes? Apparently impossible, since she didn't see them.

Maybe the weasels were hiding from her. Yeah. That was a distinct possibility. At least it was if they had the slightest inkling as to what she was thinking at the moment.

"Oh, now I'm sure this wedding is giving you ideas." Amanda patted Leigh's arm and smiled. "I can see you're studying the decorations, maybe coming up with plans for your own reception."

Leigh stared at her, stunned. Amanda was a sweet older woman, but boy, she didn't have a clue what Leigh was thinking. Not that she could exactly enlighten her. After all, how did you tell the minister's wife that you were looking for your brothers so you could kill them? Hmmm. Emily Post probably didn't have any etiquette advice for this particular circumstance.

Deciding not to go into it, Leigh said, "I'm not interested in getting married. Thanks."

Figuring that was settled, she returned to scanning the crowd. Where were those bozos? She finally spotted two of her sisters-in-law, Megan and Emma, over by the buffet table. Wherever they were, their husbands and her brothers, Chase and Nathan, wouldn't be far behind.

Bingo. She'd found them.

She started to head in that direction when Amanda once again put her hand on Leigh's arm. "Getting married and starting your own family is one of life's precious gifts," Amanda said. "As I know your brothers have discovered."

Leigh bit back a groan. Would this woman never stop? She didn't want to get married. She didn't want to fall in love.

She only wanted to talk to her ratfink brothers and then maybe kick Jared Kendrick out of here. Was that too much to ask for?

"No offense, Amanda, 'cause I know you're happily married," Leigh said. "But I have no desire to live in a house with a white picket fence."

"Do tell. Because I could have sworn that the house you're renting from Megan has a white picket fence out front," a deep voice said from behind her.

Oh, just great. While she'd been looking for her brothers, Jared Kendrick had walked up and was apparently standing directly behind her. Man oh man, this day just kept getting worse.

"Hello, Jared," Amanda said. "I heard you moved back to Honey. You're turning your parents ranch into a rodeo school, right?" Without waiting for an answer, Amanda continued, "Mary Monroe said she saw you riding that motorcycle of yours around town. And she said you were going quite fast. I told her you probably weren't, but I don't think she believed me."

Leigh rolled her eyes. Of course, the man had been driving fast. This was Jared Kendrick. If there was a rule in Honey, he broke it.

"I might have been going a couple of miles over the speed limit," Jared admitted. "Tell her I'll slow down from now on."

Unable to stop herself, Leigh snorted. "That will be the day."

"Hello to you, too," Jared said.

Turning slowly, Leigh braced herself for the wallop she knew she'd feel when she made eye contact with this man. Despite no longer liking him, she was still female. And females of all ages found it difficult to resist Jared. He was tall, over six feet, and had amazingly thick dark-brown hair and equally dark eyes. The man was serious eye candy.

Dang his hide.

Predictably, as soon as Leigh looked at him, her

DNA betrayed her. Her stupid heart raced. Her equally stupid breathing seemed to have grown rapid and shallow.

This world was one screwy place when the man you disliked more than any other turned you on like crazy.

Sheesh.

Taking a deep breath to calm her raging libido, she flashed him a completely insincere smile. "Why, hello, Kendrick. I thought you'd be in jail by now. Did the parole board take a liking to you?"

Jared laughed, the sound deep and rich and way too appealing. "Glad to see you haven't changed since last summer, Leigh."

Amanda frowned and made a tsking sound. "Oh, Jared, were you really in jail? My, my. I thought you were riding with those rodeo people. Of course, you were a trifle wild while growing up here, but I had no idea you'd run into serious trouble."

Leigh waited patiently for Jared to correct the older woman and explain he hadn't been in jail, but he simply shrugged. Oh, for the love of Pete. Was he really going to let this go? The Honey rumor mill would have a field day. Leigh knew that before the night was over, all the good folks of Honey would swear up and down that Jared had been in jail for murder.

"Maybe my husband could counsel you," Amanda offered. "He's very good with things like this."

Leigh groaned. "Amanda, Jared wasn't in jail. I was kidding."

Amanda laughed softly, and Leigh rolled her eyes.

"Oh, good. You two are joking," Amanda said. 'I'm happy to hear that. Although I will admit I was surprised to see you in the wedding party today. I didn't know you were friends with Trent."

"Everyone seemed surprised to see me," he said. "Leigh more so than most. I especially liked the way she screamed when she noticed me standing next to her brothers by the altar. You'll have to check with your husband, Amanda, but I bet she's the first bridesmaid to scream like that during a ceremony."

"Oh, pulleese. I'm sure a lot of women scream around you," Leigh said, and then she felt like whacking herself on the side of the head when she realized the interpretation that could be put on her words. From the grin on Jared's face, he'd taken it as a compliment to his lovemaking prowess.

Leigh shook her head. "Hey! Don't go there. I only meant—"

Jared held up one hand and drawled, "I know exactly what you meant, Leigh, and thanks. Maybe one day you can find out for yourself if it's true."

Keenly aware that Amanda was watching them,

Leigh said in her sweetest voice, "Kendrick, I'd rather two-step with a rattlesnake. No, wait, it wouldn't be much different, would it?"

Amanda frowned and looked from Leigh to Jared then back at Leigh. "What are you talking about, dear? Are you teasing Jared again?"

A sexy grin slowly crossed Jared's handsome face. "Yeah, Leigh, are you teasing me again?"

"I'm completely, absolutely sincere," she said firmly, which only made Jared grin more.

Typical.

"Oh." Amanda looked confused. "I see. Well, I guess we'd better find our seats now. It looks like the toasts are about to start," Amanda pointed out.

Leigh glanced around. People were quickly finding their places at the small round tables. With a quick goodbye to Amanda, Leigh headed over to the table near the front where she was supposed to sit. Now she'd have to wait until later to talk to her brothers, but at least she'd be away from Jared.

Boy, he really got to her. Big time. Why in the world had her doofus brothers invited him to be in the wedding party? Had love turned their brains to mush? They hated Jared, and ever since their dating fiasco a few months back, he was the last man she ever wanted to see again.

So what in the world was he doing here?

And why in the blazes did he still get to her so much?

⬥

Jared chuckled as he watched Leigh weave her way through the tables. She was mad at him. Really mad at him.

Good. Mad meant he still got to her. Mad meant she hadn't forgotten what had happened last summer.

Mad meant he had a good chance of making his plan work.

"It was lovely to see you again," Amanda told him.

Before the older woman could wander away, Jared jumped at the chance to secure another ally in this town.

"I really enjoyed seeing you, too," he told her. "Now that I'm going to settle down in Honey, I'm hoping the townsfolk will rethink their opinion of me." With a deliberately self-effacing smile, he added, "You know, maybe forget a couple of those wild things I did when I was a kid."

With a nod, Amanda told him, "I understand. You'd like a second chance."

"Exactly."

"Changing people's minds may take a little doing," she warned him. "I've heard quite a few stories about you. And there was that time shortly after my husband and I first moved here when someone covered all the trees in front of the church in pink toilet paper."

Okay. He deserved that. "Actually, Amanda, if memory serves me, I covered all the trees on Main Street in toilet paper not just those in front of the church. It was nothing personal. Plus, I was a kid."

She seemed surprised that he'd owned up to the prank. "Oh. Yes. I guess I knew that. Still, it was a mess."

He moved forward and told her, "I'm very sorry about the mess. And to make up for it in some small way, I hear you're collecting money to do landscaping next spring."

She blinked. "We're hoping to raise enough to plant some shrubs and maybe more flowers."

"I'd like to help. Tomorrow when I come to church, I'll give you a check to help cover those expenses."

She blinked even more. "You're coming to church? Really?"

Jared bit back a sigh. Changing everyone's opinion of him wasn't going to be easy. "Yes."

She rewarded him for his answer by giving him a sweet smile. "We'll be happy to have you. But, Jared, I hope you aren't trying to buy my goodwill."

"Of course not," he said, even though in a way he was. He had to start somewhere. If he didn't get the people in this town on his side, he'd never make a go of Kendrick Rodeo School. Deciding to be honest with Amanda, he said, "I want to be a part of this town, and from now on, you and your husband will find me sitting in church every Sunday."

"It's good to have you back. And I'm sure, with time, everyone will welcome you home." She leaned a little closer and said, "But you might want to try being nicer to Leigh. I don't think you did much to win her over tonight. She seemed very perturbed with you."

Oh, yeah, she was perturbed all right. But that was just fine with him. He'd already decided his approach with Leigh had to be different from what he used with everyone else in town. With the rest of the people, he could win them over with kindness.

But kindness wouldn't work with Leigh. Especially after what had happened last summer. No, to win Leigh over, he'd need to be a lot like her—downright sneaky.

Not that he'd share that with Amanda. He doubted she'd approve of his plan.

After saying goodbye to the older woman, he wandered over to the table near the back of the room where he'd put both his and Leigh's place cards. It wouldn't take her long to discover he'd moved them from the table near the front to this table by the back door. And once she figured it out, she'd have a fit.

Should be fun.

He leaned against his chair and waited, smiling as he watched her approach the tables near the front and search for her place card. She searched one table. Then another. Then another.

"Five, four, three, two, one..." he counted down slowly to himself. Suddenly, Leigh spun around and glared at him across the width of the room.

"Ignition." He chuckled. She looked ready to explode.

Although her slinky pink bridesmaid dress made her look like a princess, at the moment, Leigh more closely resembled a fire-breathing dragon. She literally stomped across the room until she stood directly in front of him.

"You are the lowest man on the face of the earth," she told him. "You're so low, you're whatever pond scum considers low."

He leaned close and said softly, "Flattery will get you nowhere."

Leigh made a growling noise, and he bit back another chuckle.

"Let me get this chair for you." He pulled her chair out with a flourish. "Have a seat, darlin'." She narrowed her eyes and shot him a look that could melt the skin off a lesser man. Yeow. That was one mad woman.

Good thing he wasn't a lesser man.

"Don't call me darlin', Kendrick," she said slowly. "Your charm doesn't work on me." She pulled her chair away from him and sat.

Sitting in his own chair, he turned to face her. "Seems to me that just a few months ago you liked it when I called you darlin'. Or was that only because you thought dating me would rile your brothers? Now that your brothers and I are getting along, I guess you don't like it anymore."

Leigh rolled her eyes. "I went out with you because I was delusional at the time. Must have been some sort of forty-eight-hour virus where your judgment disappears faster than a rodeo rider. And you did disappear, didn't you? Seems to me the last time we talked, you were going to take me to dinner. But you never showed."

Now this was fun. He'd missed these twelve-round verbal bouts with Leigh since he'd left Honey.

"I'm here now," he said.

She glanced at her watch. "You're about...umm, four months too late."

Leaning toward her so that no one would overhear, he said, "You're not really mad that I cut out. You didn't care a thing about me."

"Hey, that's not true. Why else would I have gone out with you?"

Jared studied her pretty face. He loved looking at Leigh. Not only was she beautiful, with silky black hair and sexy blue eyes, but she was also full of life and fire and passion. Lots and lots of passion.

But she'd never seen him as a person. She'd only seen him as a way to upset her brothers.

"You're not mad at me," he told her. "You're just mad that I wouldn't have sex with you."

She blew out a huffy sigh. "That only proves that you're totally devoid of good judgment."

He laughed. "Do tell."

"Yes. And for your information, you had the perfect opportunity, and you blew it. Your loss."

"Don't I know it," he said, laughing again when she stuck her tongue out at him. Leigh was never shy about expressing her feelings. It was one of the things he liked about her.

And there were lots of things he liked about Leigh. He'd always found her fascinating, even when they'd been kids. Leigh had a way of looking life in the eye and daring it to mess with her plan. You couldn't help but admire her spirit.

The fact that she was also gorgeous only made the

whole package that much more appealing. But he didn't appreciate being used. And Leigh had used him. She'd gone out with him because he was the bad boy of Honey. She loved to rock the boat, and being with him would have not only rocked the boat, but it would have capsized it.

So he hadn't played along. He'd never cared for being used and still didn't. If Leigh felt the need to ruffle feathers in Honey, she'd have to do it without him. His feather-ruffling days were over.

He'd moved back to town a couple of weeks ago, figuring the family ranch would be a great place to open his rodeo school. Knowing that for his school to succeed he'd need to woo the goodwill of the people of Honey, he'd started with the Barrett brothers. Each of them had proven tough to thaw, but he'd managed it.

He glanced at Leigh, and she shot him another icy stare. Looked like thawing her was going to take some doing, too.

"So how have you been?" he asked, figuring that was a safe enough topic.

She sighed. "I'm ignoring you, so don't talk to me."

"But I'm not ignoring you, so why can't I talk? I know, you ignore me, and I'll handle the conversation for both of us."

When she made no response, he asked, "So, Leigh, how have you been?"

Then in his best female voice, which he made deliberately sultry, he said, "Oh, Jared, this town hasn't been the same since you've been away. Like all the other ladies in Honey, I've missed you so much I couldn't think about anything else."

Next to him, Leigh snorted. "Get real."

He ignored her response and kept on. "Well, Leigh, I'm glad to hear you missed me. I missed you, too."

Again, she snorted, and this time shifted so her back was to him.

He used the female voice again. "Oh, Jared, did you really miss little ol' me? I'm all aflutter."

That got to her. Leigh spun around. "Aflutter? You're out of your mind. And for the record, I didn't miss you."

Again, he ignored her response and continued on. "Well, darlin', I'm glad to hear you're no longer mad about that misunderstanding we had. You know, I was tempted to take you up on your offer of hot sex, but I didn't like being used like that."

Leigh looked like a pressure cooker about to explode.

"I completely understand, Jared," he said softly in the female voice. "I should have realized it was unfair of me to ask you out for the sole purpose of making my brothers mad. I'll have to think of a way to make it up to you. Maybe I could make you dinner one night. Or help you decorate your house. Or, I know, I could make that hot sex offer again, but this time because I want you, not because I want to shake up the good folks of Honey."

Leigh jumped out of her chair, knocking it over in her haste. "In your dreams, hayseed."

Then she walked away. Actually, she stomped away. And every person in the room turned to stare at him.

Yeah, he was back in Honey all right. And it looked like his feather-ruffling days weren't completely behind him after all.

❦

The toasts were over, so people were wandering around again. Leigh finally found her brothers Chase and Nathan standing by the bar. Their wives, Megan and Emma, were across the room talking to a group of ladies, so for the moment, Leigh had the boys to herself. Good, because the three of them needed to have a little family chat.

"Hey, kiddo, great wedding, wasn't it?" Chase asked.

She wasted no time. "Why is Jared here?"

Nathan shrugged. "Who else could Trent ask when Joe got sick? We had to find someone who was the right size for the tux. I asked Jared, and he said he didn't mind helping out. He's a nice guy."

Nice? Nice?

"You're kidding, right? You don't like Jared. None of you have ever liked him," she pointed out.

Chase patted her on the shoulder. "Calm down. That's in the past. When he first moved back to town, he stopped by and talked to each of us. I don't think we made it easy on him, but he showed a lot of gumption and toughed it out. The man wants to settle here in Honey and help the town. I think we all need to give him a second chance. Nathan, Trent, and I have agreed we'd do what we could to help him."

Openmouthed, Leigh stared at her oldest brother, unable to believe what he was saying. For the first time in memory, she was at a complete loss for words. Something was definitely wrong. These couldn't be her brothers. They had to be alien clones. Her brothers wouldn't act this way.

When she finally recovered from the shock of hearing Chase call Jared nice, she sputtered, "So just like that"—she snapped her fingers—"you now like Jared where for years and years, you couldn't stand him."

Chase glanced at Nathan, then they both nodded.

"Pretty much," Chase admitted. "But you have to realize, we took to disliking Jared when we all were in high school. We're adults now. Might as well bury old hatchets."

This was unbelievable. She looked at Nathan, the most logical one of the whole Barrett family.

"A few months ago, you went out of your way to warn me against Jared. You said he was all wrong for me."

"He was. He was a rodeo rider, and we knew he'd pack up and leave town at the drop of a hat, which he did. But now he's back and trying to start a business. Got to admire a man who helps his parents out by paying top dollar to buy their failing ranch so they can retire to Florida. And he's set out to build a profitable business here, which will definitely be good for Honey."

Nathan took a couple of glasses of champagne from the bartender, then said, "You should try to be nice to him, Leigh. Jared's actually a good guy. Everyone deserves a second chance."

Before she could answer, Emma and Megan walked up, and Leigh watched both of her brothers kiss their wives.

"Hi, Leigh," Megan said, giving her a smile. "Wasn't the ceremony wonderful? Erin and Trent seem so much in love." She beamed at Chase. "Looks like all the Barrett men have found love."

"You should give it a try," Chase told Leigh. "It might help with your disposition."

"Hardeharhar," Leigh said. "My disposition is just fine, thank you very much. And I have no intention of falling in love, not when I finally have some breathing room now that you boys have your own lives to worry about."

"Suit yourself," Chase said, slipping one arm around Megan's waist. "But you don't know what you're missing."

Yeah, she did. She'd be missing out on having another person keeping tabs on her day and night. Her brothers had done enough spying to last her a lifetime. Freedom stretched out before her, and she wasn't about to give it up.

Deciding she'd gotten nowhere with her brothers, she said goodbye and wandered the room, looking for someone to take her mind off Jared Kendrick. The dancing had started, which would definitely take her mind off the man. She loved to dance, and since practically everyone in town had come to the wedding, it shouldn't be too difficult to find a willing partner.

She didn't have to look for long. Within minutes, she spotted Billy Joe Tate, a guy she'd dated a couple of times over the years. Billy didn't get her heart racing the way Jar—er, some men did, but he was a nice guy.

She tapped him on the shoulder. "Hey, Billy. Feel like dancing? They're playing our song."

At that particular moment, the band was playing a rather poor version of "Proud Mary."

Billy turned and smiled at her. "Hey, Leigh. This is our song? I didn't know we had a song. Well, except maybe the high school's anthem. You know, 'Go Mighty Panthers, pride and joy of our town. We're always there for you, even when...um, something is something something.'" He scratched his head. "Guess I don't remember all the words."

Leigh snagged his hand. Yep, Billy Joe Tate was exactly what she needed to get her mind off what's-his-name. When they reached the dance floor, she threw herself into the dance heart and soul, feeling free and alive and too happy for words. Gone were the pressures of the day. Gone were any worries. It was just the music, running through her body, feeding her soul.

When the band finished, they immediately started a slow song. Leigh reluctantly came to a halt and turned toward Billy. But his arms weren't the ones that circled her waist, and it certainly wasn't Billy's body she brushed against on the crowded dance floor.

"Where's Billy?" she asked Jared, none too happy to find herself dancing with him but deciding not to make another scene at her brother's wedding.

"His cell phone rang while you were dancing. I think he tried to tell you, but you were kinda lost in your own world. A few minutes ago, he wandered off to talk on the phone." His brown eyes twinkled with mischief. "I figured since you were out on the floor all by yourself, I'd come to your rescue."

"My rescue? What exactly do you think you're rescuing me from? Do you see any danger here?"

"You know what I mean."

"No, I'm afraid I don't." Annoyed by his attitude, a devious idea popped into her head. She placed her hands on his chest and waited until they got bumped again by other couples. Then she softly undid a few buttons on his vest. He was in for a surprise when this dance ended. A big surprise.

"From now on, Kendrick, don't do me any favors. I'm all grown up. I can take care of myself."

"For starters, I figured this was the only way you'd ever dance with me. Plus, I didn't want you to be embarrassed when you realized your dance partner had left," he said, swaying them to the soft, seductive music. "I thought I could do something nice for you."

Leigh didn't know what to make of his answer.

Frankly, it surprised her. Was he serious? Was he really trying to be nice?

She didn't know what to think anymore.

But the one thing she was sure of was that he was dead wrong about her. She wouldn't have been embarrassed.

Of course, she couldn't say the same thing for him. She bit back a smile, thinking about Jared redoing his vest in front of the crowd once the song ended.

"I don't get embarrassed," she assured him. "I'm not ashamed of the way I am. I know you think I only went out with you to upset my brothers, but that's not true."

At his doubtful look, she relented a tad. "Okay, getting my brothers riled up was a side benefit, but I went out with you because I'd always wanted to go out with you."

"So you could have sex with me," he said.

"Yeah, well, is that such a crime? You've always been wild. So what's the big deal? I didn't think guys got all huffy about stuff like that."

"So I wasn't the first guy you went out with solely for the purpose of having sex?"

She sighed. "Okay, yes, you were. But, Jared, it's not like you care. I know what you're like."

"How is that possible, Leigh? Up until our first

date, we hadn't said ten words to each other in all the years we've lived in the same town. Did you consult a crystal ball with questions about me?"

Jeez, she hated this. He was making some really good points. She hadn't considered it from his side. Maybe she shouldn't have assumed just because he was majorly cute that all he was interested in was getting lucky.

"Fine. I apologize," she said, but she didn't really like doing it. "I shouldn't have thought that just because you chase women all the time that you'd be interested in no-strings sex. How foolish of me."

"Was that an apology or an accusation?"

She laughed. "Kendrick, just settle for it, okay? And we'll agree to try to get along."

"Not much of a truce, but I guess I can live with it. Who knows? Maybe we can be friends," he said, his body warm against hers as they kept time with the music.

She'd give him this—he was a great dancer. And he smelled like heaven. So much so that it took a couple of seconds for his words to penetrate her lust-filled brain.

Friends? He wanted them to be friends?

"I'm not sure that's possible," she admitted.

"Sure it is. Just give it a try." He twirled them a

little, causing Leigh to hold him tighter. "I apologize for messing up your plans last summer."

Plans. Right. That reminded her. Maybe she needed to rethink the whole undone vest thing now that they'd come to a hazy agreement. She might not be ready to be friends with this man, but maybe she shouldn't leave him on the dance floor with his clothes undone.

Too bad that thinking of any sort was proving difficult at this particular moment. Her hormones were having a field day being held this close to Jared. Being in his arms felt amazingly good.

When they got bumped yet again, he pulled her even closer. Leaning down so she could hear him, he said, "I'm glad we had this chance to talk. I'm back now, and for lots of reasons, things didn't work out between us. But that doesn't mean we can't get along. I really am settling here for good. I'd like to know you're on my side. I'd like to know you're my friend."

Leigh looked up into his devastatingly handsome face. There was the word again—friends. He wanted them to be friends. She was the type who generally got along with everyone, so surely she could find a way to get along with Jared. Everyone else in her family seemed to be getting along with him just fine these days.

So maybe a truce was the only logical thing to do.

He skimmed the fingers of one hand slowly down her back to her waist, and she barely managed not to sigh. Friends. Was it possible to be friends with a man like Jared Kendrick? More importantly, was it possible to be friends with a man who'd repeatedly said "no" when you'd thrown yourself at him?

Um, she had to think about that one.

"I guess I can stop being mad at you," she relented. "Or at least I can try to stop being mad at you. I can't promise miracles."

"Ah, Leigh, but I'd like more. I'd like us to be people who help each other out in times of need."

Something in the way he said that made her frown. "When would we ever need to help each other?"

He leaned down until his lips were next to her left ear, then he whispered, "How about now? I'll rezip your dress if you refasten my vest."

2

She was going to end up blind, Leigh decided as she squinted against the brilliant sun flooding in through the window in the office of Gavin Monroe, principal of Honey High School. Why on earth did Gavin insist on having his desk situated so his back was to the window? She couldn't see a blasted thing.

"Leigh, I asked you to stop by today for a couple of reasons. First, I think you're doing a great job with your student teaching assignment. The kids love you, and your fellow teachers have nothing but wonderful things to say about you."

Mentally, Leigh did a little happy dance. Yippee. About time she got some good news. Ever since the wedding reception a little over a week ago, she'd been feeling out of sorts. It could have something to do with Jared besting her on the dance floor, but she doubted it. She was enough of a good sport to give him credit for that one.

No, the reason she'd felt mopey was that she'd been undeniably turned on during their dance—the one where he'd talked about being friends. It was happening all over again. She wanted Jared, but he didn't want her.

Talk about pathetic. She needed to find some sort of anti-Jared potion before she saw him again. Something that would make it so she could stand next to him without wanting to strip him naked and throw him on the floor.

Maybe the local drugstore had something. Hmm, probably not. Probably the only thing that would help was to avoid him completely.

That shouldn't be too hard. He lived out of town. She worked long hours. There was no reason for them to see each other again.

And now, judging from all the compliments Gavin was tossing her way, she was about to have a major pick-me-up. She could practically guess what Gavin's next words were going to be—he was going to ask her to join the staff full time starting next year. After all those years of college, she'd finally get to be a teacher at Honey High School.

"Thank you so much for the compliments, Principal Monroe," she said in her best teacher voice. Since Gavin was only thirty-five, the same age as her oldest brother, Chase, and they'd grown up together, it felt weird being so formal with him. She still clearly remembered him helping out at his family's drugstore and blushing like mad every time a good-looking girl walked in.

But hey, if Gavin wanted everyone to call him Principal Monroe, then that's what she'd call him.

Heck, she was willing to call him Santa Claus, if that was what he wanted. Anything to get the job.

Gavin smiled, obviously enjoying delivering the good news. "Since you've done such a good job, and you really fit in here at Honey High, I'd like..." His words trailed off, and his attention focused on something behind her.

Leigh leaned forward. *Yes? Yes? Hello.* She looked over her shoulder. What was he staring at? The picture of his wife? The clock? What?

Turning back to face him, she tried to verbally nudge him forward. "Yes, Principal Monroe?"

He blinked. "Sorry. I didn't realize it was so late."

This was getting annoying. Leigh slapped a smile on her face and said, "I'm sure our meeting is almost over. You were saying, you'd like...?"

Gavin nodded and thankfully directed his attention back to her. "Leigh, I'd like to offer you a job as—"

"Yes," she blurted.

He smiled. "So you knew what I was going to ask? I guess the school grapevine is working overtime. Well, I'm glad you know, and I'm glad you said yes."

"Frankly, I'm thrilled. This is something I've wanted for a long time." Boy, was it ever. A full-time teaching job at Honey High. Life didn't get much sweeter than this.

Before she could say anything else, the door to Gavin's office opened behind her, and Leigh heard someone walk in.

"Sorry I'm late."

The deep male voice drifted over Leigh's shoulders. Oh, no. No, no, no. What was Jared doing here? He had no business being here. How was she supposed to avoid him if he kept appearing in places he shouldn't be?

She tipped her head and looked at him. He gave her a quick wink, then walked around and sat in the chair next to her. Darn his hide; he looked gorgeous as usual. He had on jeans and a black T-shirt and looked less like a rodeo rider than a midnight fantasy.

Just great. This could not be happening. Not again. Stunned, she stared at him, but he looked at

Gavin instead. Before she could say anything, Jared held one hand up and shielded his eyes.

"Whoa, that sun sure is bright. I think I may lose my eyesight," Jared said. "Gav, mind lowering the blinds so Leigh and I can see?"

Gav? He called the principal Gav?

Apparently so, since Gavin immediately apologized and quickly closed the blinds. "Sorry about that, Jared."

"No problem." Jared grinned at Leigh. "So, what do you think? Did Gav explain the plan? Are you on board with everything?"

What did she think? Was she on board? If they were swapping questions, she had a good one—what was he doing here?

"So what do you think?" Jared prompted again.

She stared at him. "About what?"

"The job." Jared looked at Gavin and raised one brow. As much as she hated to notice, Leigh didn't miss how the sunlight still seeping in around the blind slats made his dark-brown hair shine. Jared had great hair. Soft and just long enough to give him a wild look.

Blinking, she brought her attention back to the conversation. She had to stop thinking about him that way. "Yes, I accepted the job," she said.

"Really?" Jared grinned at her. "Good. It should be fun."

Gavin leaned back in his chair. "Leigh's a great asset to the school. She already knew about the job when she got here, and she didn't hesitate a bit in accepting."

Why would she hesitate? Gavin had to know she wanted a full-time job at the school. Of course, she'd said yes. Why did they find that so unbelievable?

Uh-oh. Suspicion slowly crept through her. Something wasn't right. There was no reason for them to be surprised. Was there?

She studied them. Their smiling faces. Their happy looks. Oh, yeah, something wasn't right. Quickly running through the conversation with Gavin in her mind, she bit back a groan when she realized she'd interrupted him. He hadn't completely finished speaking when she'd said yes.

But what other job could he mean? Naturally he was talking about a full-time teaching job.

Wasn't he?

But if it was, then why was Jared here?

Shoving aside the feeling of impending doom, she said to the principal, "I'd like to know a little bit more about this job."

"Certainly." Gavin folded his hands on his desk. "Homecoming this year is being called Wild Westival.

Don't you think that's cute? The student council has arranged for the halftime show, the student dance, and the alumni dance, but that still leaves the parade. No one has time to take it on. Then Jared stepped up, solving our problem."

Leigh felt her stomach drop to the floor. Rats. This wasn't about a full-time job. Not at all. It was about a homecoming parade.

How could she have been so stupid?

Acutely aware of Jared sitting next to her, she refused to let her disappointment show. Sure, she wasn't getting the teaching job. At least, not yet. But if she helped on this Westival thingy, then she'd be a shoo-in. Gavin always rewarded employees who pitched in on extracurricular activities.

"Why Wild Westival?" she asked Jared.

He was looking at her oddly, almost as if he'd figured out that she'd been thinking along different lines when Gavin had offered the job. Well, that was her own business, and she wasn't telling him about it.

"What did you have in mind?" she prompted when he didn't answer.

He leaned toward her. "Are you okay?"

"Why wouldn't I be okay?" she countered, hating the fact that he'd sensed she was upset while her boss was sitting there completely oblivious to the fact that he'd rained on her happiness by asking her to work on the homecoming parade.

Jared refused to let the subject drop. "Did you mean to agree to help with homecoming parade or did you think Gav was talking about something else when you said yes?"

There was no way she was going to tell Jared what she'd thought. Turning the tables, she asked, "What I want to know is why you agreed to help with the parade? You don't work for the high school, so why get involved?"

"Why are both of you asking questions and neither of you is answering?" Gavin interjected.

Jared chuckled. "Sorry about that. Okay, I'll answer first. I was talking to Gav, and he mentioned there might not be a parade this year because they were short on resources. I figured I might as well help. I know how much homecoming weekend means to this town. This is Texas, and we're talking football." He grinned that famous sexy grin of his, and Leigh felt her heart rate pick up. Talk about being seriously pathetic.

He leaned toward her. "Rumor has it that there are a couple of folks who have less than stellar memories of me."

Leigh laughed. "Ya think? Maybe it has something

to do with you painting the water tower an ugly shade of lime green with neon pink stripes?"

"I had to paint over it," Jared reminded her. "Took me most of the summer. That pink was hard to cover up. I had to paint that water tower three times before you couldn't see it anymore."

Leigh remembered those days well. Jared, painting on the water tower. Often without a shirt. On any given day, you could find most of the female population of Honey hanging out at that end of town, enjoying the magnificent view.

Of course, she hadn't joined the groupies at the bottom of the water tower stairs. Nope. Not her. Instead, she'd been busy that summer acting as the receptionist for Danny Hoover, the local lawyer. She'd greeted his clients, answered his phones.

The fact that his office afforded whoever was seated at the receptionist's desk a stellar view of the water tower had just been a coincidence.

"See, Jared made up for his little prank," Gavin said. "He had to pay the price, and he did. That's all a person can do. We all make mistakes."

Gavin had to be kidding. Jared hadn't made mistakes; he'd run around like a wild man.

Unable to let this go so easily, Leigh asked, "And didn't you also switch the hubcaps on all the teachers' cars during a pep rally? It seems to me it took almost two weeks for everyone to sort out that little mistake."

Jared shrugged. "Maybe I switched a few hubcaps."

Leigh snorted, and Jared laughed.

"Hey, it's true. I couldn't get all the hubcaps off. Some of them were locked on."

Leigh knew she should drop the subject, but the truth was, she didn't want to work with Jared on a committee. She didn't want to be anywhere near him. Too much could go wrong, and she might end up making a fool of herself again. That was more than she could take.

Hoping to change Gavin's mind, she threw down her trump card. "And let's not forget you ruined the homecoming parade your senior year when you freed all the dogs from the pound and let them loose on the town."

"I guess next time I pick a friend, I'll find one with a shorter memory," Jared said, his brown eyes twinkling with humor.

Leigh knew he wasn't thrilled she was bringing up all his past indiscretions, and realistically, she couldn't blame him. Even though she hadn't signed on with that whole friend thing, she had agreed to try to get along with him. So far, she was doing a crummy job.

"But I guess you've reformed," she relented.

"When a man gets older, he starts to realize what's important in life," Gavin said in his most pompous voice. "Young people make mistakes, Leigh. If memory serves, your brothers made more than a few when they were young. And you may have made a couple yourself along the way. You should congratulate Jared for turning over a new leaf."

Personally, she wasn't completely convinced there weren't all sorts of creepy things under that leaf, but she kept her opinion to herself.

"How long do we have to organize the parade?" she asked, hoping she could find a way to do this without actually having to see Jared.

"Not quite four weeks. The plans are already underway for the dances and the homecoming show, so you may find it a challenge getting student volunteers. Maybe a few of the freshmen and sophomores would be willing to help. The juniors and seniors are already running the other committees."

That's right. They'd have student volunteers. Bodies that could help Leigh maintain her distance from Jared.

Whew. That was a relief.

Gavin leaned back in his chair. "The school really appreciates this. The parade always sets the tone for homecoming weekend and helps draw in a lot of out-of-town visitors. I know all the local merchants were disappointed when we told them there might not be a parade this year. In fact, my parents were thrilled when I told them Jared had stepped up to the plate and would make sure it happened after all. You two should have a lot of fun."

Oh, yeah, she'd bet they'd have a spiffy doodle time. She gave Gavin a wan smile. "Should be swell."

Jared chuckled. "See, Leigh's already so excited about this she's about to burst. Gavin, why don't Leigh and I go do some planning and stop back by in a few days to tell you what we've figured out?"

"Sounds good," Gavin said, then he stood and showed them to the door. Right before they walked out, he shook their hands. "Thanks again, Jared. Leigh. I really appreciate this, and I know everyone in Honey does, too. Homecoming wouldn't be the same without the parade."

Leigh barely managed to keep her mouth shut until they were out of earshot of Gavin's office. Then she stopped and looked at Jared.

"Why?"

"Why what?"

"Why are you doing this?"

He tipped his head, pretending to be confused, but Leigh didn't buy it for a second.

"I told you. I want to help the town," he eventually said.

"Why with me? You can't tell me Gavin chose me to do this. You must have suggested I help. Why me?"

"I thought we'd agreed we were friends. Who else would I ask to help me?"

That blasted friend thing again. "For the record, all I agreed to was to try to get along. That's completely different from being friends."

Jared nodded. "Okay. Good enough. We'll be people who are trying to get along working together on the parade. I'll get some good publicity out of it, and you'll convince Gav to give you a full-time teaching position. Sounds like a win-win to me."

"How do you know that's what I want?"

"You are one suspicious woman." Taking a couple of steps toward her, he explained, "Chase mentioned it at the wedding."

For a second, Leigh studied him, trying to judge his sincerity. He seemed to be telling the truth as far as she could tell. Then, without meaning to, she blurted, "I hate it when you're nice."

He looked surprised at first. Then he laughed. "Darn annoying, isn't it?"

This time, she laughed as well. "Yes. It is. I don't want to like you."

"And here I go, being so incredibly likable." He pretended to think, then said, "I know. From now on, whenever we see each other, I'll be mean and surly. How about that? Will that make it easier on you?"

"I'd take it as a personal favor," she said. She knew he thought she was teasing, but she really would appreciate it if he at least tried not to be so darn appealing.

But how did you ask a man not to turn you on?

His gaze locked with hers, and Leigh felt her pulse rate pick up. Oh, no. Not again.

Maybe she'd given up on that potion idea too soon.

Turning, she headed toward the exit. She needed to get away from him, away from his sexy smile and seductive laugh. When she reached the door, good manners and a strong sense of fair play forced her to say to him, "This is a good thing you're doing for the town. It's nice of you to help."

"Homecoming seemed like the best way to get everyone in town to realize I've changed. After all, I don't think our mutual striptease at the wedding reception swayed anyone over to my side, do you?"

He had a point. Although only the couples closest to them on the dance floor actually noticed that she and Jared had to redress themselves once the music ended, this was Honey. Gossip that juicy spread quicker than a lame joke on the Internet.

Frankly, Leigh was surprised Gavin hadn't

mentioned it today, since that seemed to be all anyone talked about these days. But no doubt the principal had kept his mouth shut because he didn't want to run the risk of chasing off two volunteers.

"No, I guess it didn't help your reputation," she said. "Didn't help mine, either." She shoved open the door but before she walked out, Jared stopped her.

"Do you think what happened on the dance floor might hurt your chance of getting a full-time job here?" he asked as they headed down the steps outside the school.

"I don't know."

"Want me to talk to Gav? I don't know if it would help, but I can try."

She glanced at him as they walked across the parking lot. "There you go, being nice again."

"Oops. Sorry," he said. "So do you want me to talk to Gav?"

Why did he care? Why was he so willing to help? And most importantly, since when did Gavin listen to Jared Kendrick?

"Is this the same Gav whose locker you filled with french fries?" she asked sweetly. "Oh, yes, and then you thoughtfully added ketchup, didn't you?"

He laughed. "There you go again with that terrible long-term memory thing. You know, most people in this town don't remember every little infraction I did. Like the water tower thing. I'd be surprised if very many people in town still remembered that."

Well, maybe the men had forgotten about it, but she'd bet most of the women remembered. Jared Kendrick without a shirt was not a sight a lady forgot.

But she wasn't going to admit that to him. All she said was, "I guess."

They'd reached her car, so she unlocked the driver's side door. Jared stopped her before she got in.

"I think we can really help each other. If we do a good job with the homecoming parade, we'll both have a better shot at getting what we want."

She studied him, her gaze slowly drifting down to his full lips. When she thought about things she wanted, one of them was to kiss Jared. She'd always wanted to kiss him, but despite her many attempts, she'd had no luck.

But she knew that wasn't what he meant, so she answered, "I guess you're right. It could show them that I'm mature and responsible, that is if I actually manage to act mature and responsible."

He bumped her with his arm. "Is it really that difficult?"

"Seems to be when I'm around you," she admitted. "You don't bring out the mature side in me."

"I'll work on that, too." He patted the pockets of his jeans. "You got a piece of paper I can use? This list is getting long. Maybe I should write it down. Let's see, I need to stop being nice. And I have to stop bringing out the immature side of you. Anything else you'd like me to do?"

Oh, now there was a loaded question. Leigh yanked open her car door and climbed inside. "I'll let you know if I think of anything," she said dryly.

He grinned, and she knew he knew what she'd been thinking. "You do that."

Yeah, right. She'd rather eat worms than hit on Jared Kendrick again.

"You have such masculine handwriting," Janet Defries cooed as Jared finished signing her up for his rodeo school. "It's so strong and forceful."

He looked at his handwriting on the registration form. It looked like chicken scratch. The woman was crazy.

"It's awful, but thanks anyway." He looked at Janet and her two friends, Tammy Holbrook and Caitlin Estes. The three of them had come racing up the driveway first thing this morning in Janet's red convertible, claiming they were dying to learn about roping and riding and "horse stuff like that." He didn't buy it for a second. Sure, these ladies were looking to rope something, but it sure as hell wasn't a calf. They were after what Leigh had been after—a good time with a bad boy.

But a student was a student, and money was money, so he'd signed them up and taken their checks. He'd teach the basics of roping and riding. But that was all. Just as Leigh had discovered, he wasn't looking to be a belt buckle prize in anyone's personal rodeo.

"So, Jared, when do you want us to start?" Janet asked, putting her hands on her hips and calling attention to the fact that there were about three inches between the bottom of her top and the top of her bottom. Her belly button and belly button earring were on full display, but rather than finding it erotic, all Jared could think about was how it must have hurt like the devil when she'd had it pierced like that. The little hoop she wore near her navel made him think of tagged cows.

He pulled his attention back to her face. "The first class starts next Saturday morning. Be sure to wear old clothes." He glanced again at her naked belly. "And, Janet, you have to be completely covered. I mean wear jeans that come to your waist, boots, and long-sleeved shirts. We're going to be busy."

Janet pouted, but Tammy and Caitlin, who weren't dressed any more appropriately than Janet, laughed.

"Guess we'll all have to buy some boring clothes," Tammy said. "Or maybe Leigh has something we can borrow. She has a closet full of them."

Jared froze. "What do you mean by that?"

His tone must have conveyed that he wasn't too thrilled with the conversation because Tammy had the good sense to look embarrassed. "You know. Since she's been teaching, she's wearing old-lady stuff. I can't imagine why Billy Joe Tate asked her out."

That bit of information distracted Jared from the comment about Leigh's clothes. "Leigh's going out with Billy?"

Janet must have noticed the undercurrent in his voice, because she came over to stand next to him. "Billy told me he was taking her to dinner tonight at Roy's Cafe. And then after that, he's going to let nature take its course."

"Why in the blazes would he say that?" Jared asked, then felt like kicking himself for saying anything. Janet arched one well-plucked eyebrow.

"Jared, honey, you sound almost like you care," she practically purred. She placed one hand on his right arm and squeezed. "But that can't be true since you dumped Leigh last summer. I heard she undid your vest at the wedding because she was mad at you for breaking up with her, and you unzipped her dress to get her back."

Yeah, that was pretty much what had happened. When he'd first felt her undoing the buttons on his vest, he'd thought her motive was desire. Then he'd quickly realized that her actions had nothing to do with desire and everything to do with revenge.

Typical sneaky Leigh. Oddly enough, that was one of the things he liked about her. The woman was never without a plan.

"I don't care who she goes out with. I just think Billy Joe's a jerk for saying something like that," he maintained.

Caitlin Estes, the owner of the local ice cream shop and a notorious flirt, said, "The heck with Leigh and Billy Joe. I want it on the record that you can feel free to unzip my dress whenever you want."

All three of the ladies giggled at that one, but Jared was too preoccupied to care. Leigh was going to dinner with Billy Joe Tate? Was she crazy? Billy was a nice enough guy but not exactly the sharpest spur in the county.

Janet leaned toward him, her stance deliberately provocative. "You want to go to dinner with me tonight to take your mind off Leigh?"

"I'm not interested in Leigh," he told her,

knowing if he said anything different, Janet would go out of her way to sabotage his plans.

"I see," Janet said, but he knew she didn't believe him. Tough. He wasn't about to tell Janet that he was interested in Leigh. But the truth was, he'd always been interested in her.

He glanced at Janet, Tammy, and Caitlin. He sure didn't have any allies in this group. They were looking at him like he was prime rib on sale.

No, if he wanted allies, he'd have to see if Leigh's brothers might be willing to help him out. After all, his intentions toward their sister were honorable.

Unfortunately, that was the part that made Leigh so mad at him.

"So you want to go to dinner," Janet asked again. "I'll buy." When Caitlin and Tammy protested, she added, "They can come along, too."

"I don't think so," Jared said.

All three women crowded around him, and he felt as trapped as a trussed-up calf.

"You sure you won't change your mind?" Janet ran one red-painted nail down his chest. "We'll have a great time."

Jared shook his head and gently pushed his way out of the group. "No. Sorry, ladies."

All three women tried to change his mind, but he

didn't waver. He had plans tonight. Plans he wasn't about to change.

He intended on hanging out at the cafe, no matter how long it took. Sooner or later, Leigh and Billy Joe Tate would show up. Then he'd see what he could do about putting the kibosh on this whole nature-taking-its-course idea.

He hadn't moved back to town and started this rodeo school just to watch the woman he wanted fool around with some other guy.

He hadn't been thrown from that many horses.

3

"**S**o now I'm figuring there's a problem with the fuel injection system on my car instead of the radiator," Billy Joe Tate said, drawing yet another picture of who-knew-what on his napkin.

They were at Roy's Cafe, waiting to order. This date with Billy was Leigh's first crack at enjoying her newfound freedom. Of course, it might have been a little easier to enjoy if he stopped rattling on about his car, but still, freedom was freedom, even if it did come with a few boring stories. And with any luck, tonight would take her mind off Jared.

She glanced at Billy, who at the moment was tucking his napkin into his collar. Okay, maybe he wouldn't completely take her mind off Jared, but being here beat the heck out of sitting at home.

Desperate to change the subject, Leigh asked, "So have you decided what you'd like to eat?"

Billy nodded. "Chicken fried steak, same as every time I come here. It's good for the soul."

Ick. But bad for the arteries. Fortunately, Billy's coronary health was none of her business. "I think I'll have a salad."

"Chick food," Billy said with a laugh.

"Intelligent food," Leigh corrected. "Some of us want to live to see fifty."

Billy frowned. "Fifty what?"

Grrr. "Forget it."

"Wish I could forget about my car," Billy said, circling right back into the same old conversation. "Like I said, this time, I think I've finally figured out what's wrong. And once I take the system apart, maybe I'll also see where that spare part I have should go."

Oh, pulleese. Billy was a menace. Maybe she should talk to her brother Trent, the chief of police, and see if they could issue a restraining order keeping Billy at least 150 yards away from anything mechanical.

Loyalty to her fellow human beings forced her to say, "Give it up, Billy. You don't know what you're doing, so you may create even more problems than you're trying to fix. You may even make your car unsafe, which could end up hurting some innocent person. You need to get a mechanic involved."

Billy squinched up his face and looked like he planned on arguing the point, so Leigh added, "Do it for me. Please?"

That worked. He grinned. "Sure, Leigh. I'd hate for you to worry about me. I'll take my car to a mechanic and get it done right." Brightening, he added, "And this way, I'll have plenty of time to work on my phone. There's something wrong with it. A little tweak or two should fix it right up."

Leigh made a mental note not to take any phone calls from Billy in the near future. Who knew what damage he could do when he tore apart his phone? On the bright side, at least he wouldn't be driving it around town.

She opened her mouth to once again tell Billy to be careful, but before she could say anything, someone else jumped in.

"Be careful when you take apart that phone. You could hurt yourself."

Leigh spun around. Sure enough, Jared Kendrick sat at the table directly behind them. He was pretty much hidden by the huge potted fern between the two tables, but still, why hadn't she seen him sooner?

This couldn't be happening yet again. "What are

you doing here? Can't I go anywhere without you showing up?"

"I'm having dinner, and for the record, I was here first." He leaned a little to the right and waved. "Hey, Billy."

"Hey, Jared," Billy said. "You all by yourself?"

Oh, no. No, no, no. Billy couldn't be planning on doing what he sounded like he was planning on doing.

"Billy, it doesn't matter if Jared is by himself," Leigh said sweetly. "We're on a date. We should be alone."

When Billy gave her a doofy smile, she thought he'd understood her not-at-all-subtle message that she didn't want Jared to join them. They might have reached a truce, but that didn't mean she wanted to spend any more time with Jared than the homecoming parade forced on her.

But apparently, Billy didn't get her hint, because not two seconds later, he said to Jared, "Leigh and I don't mind. You should join us. I can tell you about my car."

Jared stood and walked over to their table. "Leigh, is this okay with you?"

He expected her to say no. She could see it on his face. Well, if he was going to be mature and adult and reasonable about their relationship, then darn it, she was, too.

Still, all she could manage was, "It's fine. Sit."

Of course, Jared decided to sit in the chair next to her. Now the two of them were sitting together, and Billy was across the table. To the casual observer—not that there were any casual ones in Honey—it looked like she and Jared were together, and that Billy had joined them.

Sheesh.

Billy, however, seemed as happy as a dog with a steak. He launched back into his fuel injector story and continued along that vein on and off throughout dinner. Once or twice either she or Jared tried to negotiate the conversation away from Billy's car, but he stuck to that topic and refused to budge.

Finally, in what seemed to be desperation, Jared said, "So, Billy, enough about your car. Did you ask Leigh how her day was?"

Billy blinked. "Why? She taught school, like she always does during the week."

"But I'm sure she'd like to talk about her day, too," Jared said.

Wearing a stunned expression, Billy asked, "You did something interesting today, Leigh? But you were at school. School's boring."

Okay, there was only so much a woman could take. She needed Billy to rise to the occasion and be the perfect date in front of Jared, and instead, he was doing a terrific impersonation of a dweeb.

Biting back a groan, she said, "School went very well today. The class I'm in is wonderful. In fact, quite a few of the kids are accelerated."

Billy scratched his head. "I think you should tell Gavin about that. They don't like the kids takin' stuff."

"No, no. I don't mean accelerated in that sense," Leigh said. "I just meant they're ahead of the rest of the class."

Billy bobbed his head. "Gotcha. So you should tell them to slow down and wait for everyone else. Man, I hate it when people run ahead and leave you in the dust. The kids on the track team used to do that to us all the time. It stunk."

Leigh stared at Billy, wondering why on earth she'd asked him out in the first place. A snicker from Jared quickly reminded her. Oh, yeah, she'd been hoping Billy could distract her.

Billy chose that moment to burp.

Sheesh.

"Speaking of going fast, how do you like your new car, Leigh? It's sweet. What kind of mileage do you get?"

She could tell Jared found all this oh-so amusing. Heck, she'd find it funny, too, if it wasn't all playing out in front of Jared. Life was against her. There were no two ways about it.

"Billy, why don't you ask Leigh about the work she's doing on the homecoming parade?" Jared asked.

A wide grin grew on Billy's face. "You're helping with homecoming? Cool." He turned to Jared. "Remember that time you snuck into the other team's locker room and curled the fur on their costume? The mascot came out at halftime and looked like a kitty cat rather than a ferocious lion."

Billy made a loud guffawing noise. "Man, that was sweet. None of the moms wanted us kids to go around you after that. You were trouble, they all said. Even my mom said I needed to stay away, and she let me eat cake for dinner."

"I was young," Jared said. "But people change, Billy."

"Dang, I hope not. I thought since you'd come back to town, you'd liven things up. Like that time you put orange food coloring in the school fountain. That was a hoot."

Leigh glanced at Jared. Although he was smiling, she knew he wasn't happy that Billy was trotting out his escapades.

Of course, she'd done the same thing during the meeting with Gavin, but this was different. Billy was acting like Jared couldn't have possibly outgrown his wild days, while she'd mentioned some of Jared's past antics because she'd wanted to…ah, darn it, there was no difference. She was as bad as Billy.

He burped again. Okay, maybe she wasn't quite as bad, but she was close.

Ignoring the headache she was rapidly getting, she decided to steer Billy in a new direction. "Why don't we talk about the homecoming parade? Hey, I have an idea. You should enter a float. A lot of local businesses are."

Billy frowned. "I own a dairy. What could I enter?"

Leigh thought for a minute, and then decided he could enter a decorative banner. "What about a—"

"Big, fat cow," Billy said, as if he really believed that's what Leigh had been about to say. "I could use my car, if it's fixed by then. I could ride around inside it." He snickered. "Kinda like I'd been eaten by a cow."

"Um, okay, that sounds good," Leigh said, shooting a perplexed look at Jared, who was obviously trying not to laugh.

Billy nodded. "Yep, it should be sweet. I can tie a few tarps to my car and paint them to make the cow body." He tipped his head. "I wonder what I should use for the udders."

Jared laughed. Really loud. Leigh tried not to, but

it was impossible. Even Billy laughed.

"I have no suggestions," Jared finally managed to say, wiping his eyes. "None at all."

"Yeah, me neither," Billy said. Apparently deciding to give that one some thought, he added, "Homecoming is such a blast. Remember that game our senior year when Jeff threw you that sweet pass, but that bozo from Greenville tried to snag it away from you? Man, I slammed into that kid so hard his grandparents felt it."

"Billy, I don't think Leigh wants to talk about football," Jared said.

Oh, now he was wrong there. "Pulleese. This is Texas. I always want to talk about football. But for the record, Jared barely caught that pass because he was too busy checking out the other team's cheerleaders."

When Billy chortled, Leigh added, "And you didn't slam into that kid from Greenville on purpose. Your helmet slipped so you couldn't see, and you hit him by mistake."

Both men stared at her. Jared recovered first. "You were at that game?"

"Of course. I have three brothers, all of whom played ball for Honey. I never miss a Honey Panthers home game."

Jared arched one brow. "Why does your liking

football not surprise me?"

"You'd make a great tackle," Billy assured her. "You'd be the kind who hunted down the person with the ball and didn't let them get away. You'd smush them into a big ol' pile of..." He blinked, obviously thinking. Finally, he said, "A pile of smushed person."

Now wasn't that a wonderfully flattering compliment from a man she was dating.

"Nice to know I'm the type of woman who would hunt someone down and smush them," she said dryly. "Gee, thanks."

Her sarcasm was lost on Billy. He just smiled. "You're welcome."

Next to her, she heard Jared stifle another laugh. "Don't you have someplace you need to be?" she asked him. Her exasperation meter was pretty much off the scale tonight. Much more of this and she'd go running out into the street screaming.

For his part, though, Jared looked perfectly content. "I'm in no hurry to leave. In fact, I can visit with you two all night. Thanks for your concern, though."

Leigh shot him a frown, but he only winked in return. He knew good and well what he was doing, but she couldn't figure out why he was doing it. Jared had made it clear he had no interest in her, so why the me-and-my-shadow routine? She'd finally gotten her freedom from her brothers, and now she had to put up with Jared tailing her?

As if.

Inspiration struck her. "Come on, Billy, let's head to my place. I'm renting Megan's old house now that she and Chase are married. Want to see how I've decorated the inside?"

Billy shrugged. "Not really. I'm not much on decorating. So, Jared, why didn't you ever go pro? You had magic hands."

That was it? She offered to show Billy her "decorating," and he'd rather discuss football with Jared? The man didn't deserve his Y chromosome.

She could feel Jared looking at her, waiting for her response. No doubt he found this funny. After all, he'd also turned her down when she'd offered to show him her "decorating."

What was it with the men in this town?

Okay, to be honest, Billy probably hadn't understood what she'd meant by decorating. Subtle hints tended to zoom right over his head.

But Jared had completely understood her when she'd made her desires clear to him. He'd known he'd been invited to do a lot more than comment on the color of her drapes, but he'd said no.

Pfft!

Well, she didn't care anymore. About any of it.

She'd wasted enough time with these two men tonight. She could have stayed home and defrosted her non-frost refrigerator and had a better time.

"Billy, I'm going to walk home now," she said, standing. "You can stay here and shoot the breeze with Jared."

"Um, okay," Billy said. "Can I have your dessert then? Apple pie is my favorite."

He sure sounded crushed that she was leaving. That whole running-through-the-street screaming thing was starting to look like a real possibility.

"Sure," she told him, beyond caring anymore. "Eat the rest of my dessert. Talk to Jared about football. Figure out how to turn your car into a giant cow. Whatever."

Billy grinned. "Okay."

That was the last time she'd waste any time on Billy Joe Tate. He was officially off her list of men with whom she could enjoy her freedom.

With as much dignity as she could muster, she headed out the door and started toward her house. It was only a little after eight, so a lot of people were still wandering around downtown. Thankfully, none of them stopped to talk to her. She wasn't in the mood tonight.

She'd only made it half a block when she heard Jared holler from behind her. "Leigh, wait up." He had to be kidding. Well, she wasn't stopping. No way. Deliberately, she picked up her pace.

Within a couple of seconds, though, he was even with her. "Are we power walking?" he asked when she made no move to slow down. "Because if we are, shouldn't we swing our arms?"

He demonstrated and looked so downright silly when he did it that Leigh had to slam her mouth closed to keep from laughing. How could he be so annoying, and yet, so amusing at the same time?

It wasn't fair.

"You're not going to make me forgive you," she told him once she had herself under control again. "You ruined my date on purpose."

"You didn't say good night to me." He had a wide grin on his face. "Guess we're even."

That got her. She stopped and turned to face him. "You're kidding, right?" When he shook his head, she asked, "Why should I say good night to you? You weren't my date. I didn't ask you to join us. Go have Billy say good night to you."

Jared chuckled. "He's too busy not only eating your dessert, but also mine. And when I left, he was polling people in the cafe for suggestions about the cow thing. Steve Myerson said he should use plastic trash bags, but Kenny Herbert said they'd drag on the ground."

Leigh sighed. Why did these things keep happening to her? More importantly, why did they keep happening in front of Jared? Tonight was supposed to be fun. Instead, it had become a fiasco. No, wait, a debacle. Yes, definitely a debacle.

She glanced at Jared, who was smiling at her. Leigh groaned. "Good night. There, I've told you good night, so you can go away." She started walking again. Not surprisingly, Jared fell into step next to her.

"So did you enjoy your evening with Billy?" Jared asked after they'd walked a while. "I had a good time, but I thought he burped too much."

"I would have had fun, but this incredibly rude guy butted into our date and spoiled the whole evening."

"What nerve." He lightly bumped his arm against hers. "You weren't really going to take Billy back to your place and show him your decorating, were you? I mean, the guy singlehandedly disproves Darwin's Survival of the Fittest theory."

Leigh laughed, then abruptly sobered. "Stop it. Stop it right now. Don't be nice now that you ruined my date."

Once again, he bumped her arm. "Come on. I didn't really ruin your date, did I? I thought I was helping. You didn't seem to be having a very good time with Billy."

No, she hadn't been. But that still didn't give Jared the right to butt in.

"Why are you following me?" she asked.

He glanced around. "I'm not following. I'm walking next to you. It's entirely different. If I were following you, I'd wear a trench coat, maybe some dark glasses, and definitely a hat."

Grrr. "You know what I mean, so don't play dumb. You keep showing up wherever I am. The wedding. The homecoming thing. Now dinner." She narrowed her eyes. "What are you up to?"

His expression was completely sincere as he said, "Not one thing. Guess it's fate or something."

Leigh snorted. "As if. You're up to something as sure as a pig likes to roll in mud."

Jared grinned. "Interesting analogy."

"Appropriate. And just so you know, sooner or later, I'll figure out what you're up to."

He bumped her arm yet again. "Leigh, no offense, but we live in a town the size of a postage stamp. How can we avoid seeing each other?"

His explanation sounded reasonable enough, but she couldn't shake the feeling there was more going on here. But what? And more importantly, why? What possible motivation could Jared have?

"Besides, we're friends now," he said. "We should be happy to see each other. And since we're friends, if you want me to go talk to Billy, I will. I'm sure he'd love to go out with you again."

"That's okay. I don't think Billy's what I'm looking for after all." She kept walking, wishing he'd leave her alone.

"You didn't answer my question," he said after they'd walked for a few minutes in silence.

She glanced at him. "Which one? You ask so many it's hard to keep track."

He stopped walking. "You weren't really going to ask Billy home, were you?"

"Just because you weren't interested in me doesn't mean no man is interested. For your information, there were many, many times back in high school when I had to pry Billy off me. He may be more interested in dessert than in wild sex these days, but he's not the only fish in the sea. Nor is he the only guy in Honey."

"Hey, I know you'll have no trouble finding a whole string of guys to show your decorating to," he said. "Heck, I know quite a few from my rodeo days who'd jump at the chance."

"Kendrick, you're being deliberately obtuse."

Jared scratched his jaw. "Is that anything like

being oblique, 'cause I'm sure I've been that a couple of times as well."

Leigh snorted. "You're confusing oblique with elongated."

Jared hooted a laugh. "Dang, Leigh, I can't believe you said that."

Well, she couldn't, either. And the more he laughed, the harder she had to try not to laugh, too. But he wasn't going to do this to her. He wasn't going to make her forgive him for butting into her life.

Once she'd finally gotten herself under control, she said, "I'm not looking for a bunch of meaningless affairs. But I would like to enjoy my freedom. For my entire life, I've had one brother or the other breathing down my neck. Now that they're all happily settled, I'd like to enjoy myself. Go out, have some fun."

In the fading evening light, she couldn't quite see him clearly. It made it difficult to tell what he was thinking, since Jared didn't always say exactly what was on his mind.

"But wasn't that why you hit on me? Just to have sex?" he asked.

She shrugged and gave the only explanation she had. "You got my brothers in a lather, and besides, you're cute."

"Ah. Nice to know I'm cute." He started walking

again.

She groaned loud and long. "Don't pretend to be insulted. You are cute, and you know it."

"So does that mean you're going to ask me out again, now that you have your freedom?"

She shook her head. "Nope. I'm still not interested in something serious, which is what I gather you want."

"What makes you think that?" he asked.

"You told me."

"When?"

"When I tried to kiss you on our last date. You said you weren't going to have sex with me just so I could make my brothers mad. You also said you were at a different point in your life than I'm at, and that you weren't looking for a fling."

He nodded. "I meant that. I still do."

"Fine, I understand." Her headache now felt like there were football players holding a scrimmage in her brain. She rubbed her left temple. "Good luck finding what you're looking for."

"Thanks. Hey, maybe you can help. Know any women in town looking for a serious relationship who might go out with me?"

Leigh stared at him. Hello? What universe was she in? Jared wanted her to fix him up with other women?

When she finally recovered enough to speak, she asked, "You're kidding, right? Ha, ha. Very funny."

Jared shook his head. "Of course, I'm not kidding. Your brothers told me what a great job you did finding the perfect women for them. I thought that since we're friends, you might be willing to help me out, too."

Leigh continued to stare at him, trying to figure out how she hadn't noticed until now that the man was flat-out crazy.

"You're kidding, right?" she repeated when she realized he was waiting for her answer.

Jared laughed and assured her. "Don't be so surprised. Since we're friends, naturally, I'd ask for your help. And hey, like I said, if you want me to hook you up with some of the rowdier boys from the rodeo circuit, just say the word."

"No," she told him firmly.

"No to which part? No, you don't want to help me, or no, you don't want me to hook you up with some of the guys?"

How aggravating could one man be? Scratch that. She knew how aggravating a man could be because she had the world's most aggravating one standing right in front of her.

"No to both ideas," she said.

Jared sighed. "I'm sure sorry to hear that. I was hoping you'd help me." He leaned closer and said softly, "I'm not exactly the most popular person in town. A lot of women may be reluctant to go out with me, considering the kinds of things I got up to as a kid."

Leigh was trying to follow what he was saying, but it was darn near impossible with him standing this close. The man smelled like heaven, like sandalwood and the outdoors. And when he spoke softly, like he was now, a woman couldn't help thinking about satin sheets and warm nights and wild sex.

For a nanosecond, she allowed herself the luxury of simply enjoying the experience. Then she gave herself a good, hard mental whack upside her head.

"I'm positive you won't have any trouble getting the ladies in this town to go out with you," she said, cringing when her voice came out sounding breathless and squeaky.

"Yeah, but they'll be like you. Only wanting to find out if all the stories of my sexual escapades are true. I want to go out with nice women interested in a relationship," he said. "So will you help me?"

Leigh held up one hand. She needed a minute to get her brain to let go of that whole sexual escapades idea he'd brought up.

She wasn't having much luck, what with him using

his soft voice and all, and Jared was obviously getting impatient.

"Leigh, stop staring at me like you're picturing me swinging naked from a chandelier. I'm asking you for help."

Now why'd he go and say that part about the chandelier? More importantly, why'd he go and say that part about being naked? She was only human.

"You're not going to help me," he said finally. "I can tell."

Leigh snapped. "Fine. Fine. Don't pout. I'll help you. But I still think you're being silly. No one is going to hold what you did in high school against you."

"You did. You brought up all that stuff during the meeting with Gavin."

Oops. Okay, he had her there. But still, he was wrong. "But other people won't."

"Billy did."

"Yeah, well, he also ate both our desserts. No one who's not crazy will."

Jared chuckled. "I'll let it slide that you just put yourself in that crazy category."

Based on everything that had happened during the last couple of days, that seemed to be where she belonged. They'd reached her house, so she headed up the walkway. "Have a nice night."

He put one hand on her arm. "Hey, wait a minute. So you will help me, right? Any ideas who I should ask out first?"

Leigh blew out a breath of disgust. When she'd agreed earlier, she'd only said yes to close the subject. She hadn't actually intended on finding him dates, maybe just make it appear that she was finding him dates.

But now she realized he actually expected her to find real dates for him. What to do, what to do.

She always tried to be a good friend and help out other people. And it really wasn't Jared's fault that the two of them didn't want the same things out of life. Both of those were great reasons for her to agree to help.

Of course, on the other hand, she'd rather slow dance with a grizzly bear than set Jared up with other women. She wanted him to want her. Naked, with or without the chandelier.

Jared waved one hand in front of her face. "Hello, Leigh, are you still with me?"

Leigh gave him a narrow-eyed look. "Give me a sec. I'm thinking."

Jared started whistling. "Let me know when you're done thinking."

"Cute."

He winked. "You already told me that, but thanks again."

When he started whistling again, Leigh opened her mouth to tell him to cut it out, when suddenly, a blast of inspiration hit her. If she got to pick the women he dated, she could make certain they were completely wrong for him.

Ooooh. Now this was a plan with possibility. "Sure. I have an idea," she said. "Ask out Maureen Sturham. She moved to town a couple of months ago. She's single and very nice."

To her complete amazement, Jared hugged her. Really hugged her, not one of those quick friend hugs. Nope, this was a full-body contact hug with lots of oomph.

Never one to miss a chance, Leigh hugged him back. Yep, this friend thing could definitely work to her advantage.

"Thanks," Jared told her when he moved to release her. "I appreciate it."

Then, even more amazingly, he kissed her left cheek, and slowly, carefully slid his mouth across her lips, lingering there a long, long time before he finally dropped another kiss on her right cheek.

When he finally moved away from her, Leigh gaped at him.

"Excuse me, but what was that?" Leigh could feel

her lips tingling, her heart racing in her chest. She wasn't complaining, not by a long shot, just confused. "You. Kissed. Me."

Jared shrugged. "On the cheeks. Nothing wrong with that. We're friends."

"Oh, no. That wasn't a kiss between friends. You kissed my lips, too," she pointed out, not sure whether she was accusing him or congratulating him but baffled all the same.

He shrugged. "By accident. I was only trying to get from one cheek to the other. Seemed like the best way to go about it."

With a wave, he headed back up her walkway. "Anyway, I'll see you Wednesday night at the parade-planning meeting. And thanks again for your help. I'll give Maureen a call."

"I must be crazy," Leigh muttered under her breath as she watched him leave.

When he reached the sidewalk in front of her house, he turned briefly and said, "Oh, and for the record, I don't think you're crazy."

Then he walked away.

For the longest time, Leigh just looked after him. Then she snorted and said to herself, "I'm going to help the man I want to have an affair with find the woman of his dreams. If that's not crazy, I don't know what is."

4

J ared entered the high school gym exactly eight minutes late for the parade committee meeting. That should give Leigh enough time to get aggravated, and nothing was more fun than an aggravated Leigh. Plus, it guaranteed he was in the forefront of her mind.

That fit perfectly in his plan. So far, he'd gotten Leigh to agree to be his friend. Now, he was going to make certain he was the only man she thought about.

And based on her choice of date for him, she wasn't exactly trying to fix him up, either.

Sooner or later, he was certain she'd come to realize they were perfect for each other. He knew she was the right one for him. And she'd soon figure out she needed someone in her life who could go toe-to-toe with her.

The town might not like him signing himself up for the job, but he was determined to be the man Leigh needed and deserved. No matter what it took.

As soon as he walked into the gym, he spotted Leigh. She stood in the middle of a group of people who were all talking at the same time. When she noticed him, she put a couple of fingers in her mouth and let out an ear-deafening whistle.

"Okay, now listen up. I need all those people who are interested in walking in the parade, regardless of what they want to be dressed like, to go to the left side of the gym."

A couple of people started to argue, but she quelled them with a stern look. "I know, I know, the Mime Society wants to go before the clowns, but the people dressed like panthers think they should go before everyone. I got it."

She turned her back and looked at the rest of the group. "Those of you wanting to create floats go to the right side of the gym, and for goodness' sake, do a reality check. You can't drive a float down the street if you can't see out of the windows. Period. No negotiations. I'm not having you run over the crowd just so you can fulfill your artistic vision."

Once again, a few people started to argue, but Leigh made a kind of growling noise, and everyone wandered off in the direction she'd indicated.

Then she turned her attention to him. She crossed the room and when she was a couple of feet from him, said, "You're late."

"Sorry. I was on the phone with Maureen. She wanted to talk about our date last night."

Leigh's expression made it clear she was surprised he'd moved so quickly. "I gave you her name on Monday, and you went out with her on Tuesday. You don't waste any time."

"Neither does Maureen." He took a step closer to her. "And I guess it comes as a total surprise to you that Maureen is sixty-two. She's a delightful woman with two sons who are both older than I am."

Leigh bit her bottom lip, and he knew she was trying not to laugh. "She's sixty-two? I had no idea. Well, don't worry. Women reach their sexual peak later than men. I'm sure you two will hit it off."

"Afraid we won't. She called me right before I came over here to tell me that her sons disapprove of her dating me, so we'd better not go out again."

Leigh made a sputtering sound. "Really? You poor thing."

"Mmm. Yes, well, I agreed it was for the best." He took another step closer to her. "I thought you were going to help me find someone right for me."

Tears were forming in Leigh's eyes, obviously from trying not to laugh. "I am."

He made the snorting noise she liked so much and said, "As if."

Like a dam giving way, laughter burst out of Leigh. Long, loud laughter. Jared stood patiently while she laughed. And laughed. Wheezed a little. Then laughed some more.

Although he'd do his best to pretend to be mad, he was thrilled she'd set him up with a bogus date. That meant Leigh didn't want him to find Ms. Right any more than he wanted her to enjoy her freedom with any other guy.

His plan was percolating along nicely.

After a couple of minutes, he sighed. "Okay, okay. Enjoy laughing. And from now on, I expect you to fix me up with women my age."

Leigh bobbed her head. "Sure. Okay. Sorry."

"Sorry my—" He glanced around the gym. Everyone was watching them, no doubt listening to every word they said. "Appaloosa."

Leigh must have also noticed they were the center of attention because she took a deep breath and said, "Let's get started with this meeting. Go find Tommy and Kate."

He nodded toward the crowd. "First, tell me, why are most of the store owners here? Usually only a few enter the parade."

"Not this year. This year, it seems like almost

everyone wants to either walk in the parade or enter floats. Apparently, Billy has been going around town bragging that he's going to drive a cow, and so now they want to do the same thing."

Jared studied the group, many of whom were shooting dirty looks his way. Man. Memories died hard in this town. "They want to decorate their cars like something you milk?"

"At this point, truthfully, I'd settle for more cows," she said. "Based on a couple of the ideas I've already heard, Billy's cow may be the tamest one in the whole parade. Did you know Pete Tunney wants to enter a giant toilet to represent his plumbing company? And Lilah Pearson wants to enter a coffin to represent the funeral home."

"Yuck."

"Exactly." She sighed. "Billy's cow is looking better and better. Now will you go find Tommy and Kate so we can start this meeting?"

Jared stood quietly waiting for Leigh to remember that he still had no idea who Tommy and Kate were, let alone where to look for them. Leigh was scanning items scribbled on a piece of paper, and it took a while for her to realize he was still standing in front of her. When she finally looked up, he smiled.

"What's a Tommy-and-Kate?" he asked sweetly.

She sighed. "The student volunteers on this

committee. I sent them to get a flip chart, but so far, they're about as much help as..."

"Udders on Billy's car?" Jared suggested.

Leigh groaned. "Yes. About as helpful as that. Can you go find them? They should be the only teenagers wandering around this time of night."

Before he could say anything else, a disagreement broke out on the left-hand side of the gym. Two of the store owners had the same idea of dressing all their employees up as panthers, and apparently, they were willing to fight for the right.

"My ladies will make wonderful panthers," maintained Patty Stanley of Patty's Powder and Primp.

"You'll make sissy panthers," bellowed Bud Knuke of Bud's Boats and Bait. "My boys will be so ferocious, they'll scare off real panthers."

Jared leaned over and murmured to Leigh, "His boys can do that without even being in costume."

Leigh sighed. "It's going to be a long night. Go find Tommy and Kate so we can get this over with."

Seemed like a simple enough task. "Sure. I know all the nooks and crannies of this school."

"Yeah, and you've gotten lucky in quite a few of them, haven't you?"

"Oh, now, I thought we'd agreed to play nice," he pointed out.

Leigh rolled her eyes. "Fine. Fine. I'll no longer fix

you up with women twice your age, and I'll no longer bring up the fact that in high school, you scored more than the football team. Just go find them."

Jared chuckled. Yep, he was getting to her all right. He was about to head off when she said, "Please."

Turning, he raised one eyebrow and gave her a slight smile. Then he tapped his ear and said, "I must be hearing things. I thought for a second you said please, but I know that can't be true. You'd never say please to me." He paused, then deliberately added, "Unless, of course, we were naked in bed."

As he predicted, that got to her. She snorted and said, "Like I keep telling you, in your dreams, Romeo."

"You bet. Every night." Then before she could throw something at him, and he was pretty sure she would, he walked out of the gym and went to find the teenagers.

Even though Leigh didn't hint that Tommy and Kate were anything other than student helpers, he couldn't shake the feeling that those two weren't wandering the halls looking for supplies. Every kid in school knew where the second-floor supply closet was. It didn't take but a couple of minutes to get a flip chart.

But if you intended on doing something more creative in that closet, like maybe getting a little romantic, well, that could take some time.

Whistling softly, he took the stairs two at a time. When he reached the second floor, he silently made his way down to the supply room door.

Then he banged on it as loudly as he could.

"Cut it out in there," he hollered, smiling at the scream he got in return.

Oh, yeah. Those two weren't out looking for supplies.

Figuring he'd give them a couple of minutes to compose themselves, he wandered back toward the stairwell. Then he waited.

And waited.

And waited.

Finally, the door to the supply room opened a fraction of an inch. They must not have been able to see him, because with a lot of whispers, a slim blond girl and a bulky brown-haired boy snuck out of the closet.

They turned toward the stairs, then skittered to a stop when they saw him.

"Well, hello there," Jared said. "Let me guess; you're Tommy and Kate. Ms. Barrett told me you were getting her a flip chart." He glanced at their empty hands. "But it looks like you've forgotten it."

Both kids blushed. Tommy sprinted back to the closet, presumably to get the missing flip chart. Kate stayed behind, her attention fixed on her sneakers.

Jared left her alone until Tommy got back with the chart. Then he said, "I'm Jared Kendrick. I'm going to be working on the committee with Ms. Barrett and you. That is if you remember to actually come to the meetings from now on."

Tommy took a protective step in front of Kate. "I'm Tommy Tate, and this is Kate Monroe. We were just...I mean, we just..."

Jared held up one hand. He didn't want to hear whatever excuse the boy was going to give him. Truthfully, he was having trouble getting over who these kids were.

He studied Kate. "You're principal Gavin Monroe's daughter? Little Katie?"

She nodded. "Yes."

Oh, this was too precious for words. Jared barely caught himself from laughing. Gavin had always been the straitlaced kind. The kind who never broke a single rule.

And who, Jared would guess, had no idea his daughter was hanging out in supply closets with Tommy Tate.

The urge to laugh was getting stronger, so instead, he nodded toward the girls' room. "I think you should go clean up, Kate, before we go downstairs. Your grandmother and grandfather are at the meeting. If you go in there looking the way you do, they'll know what you've been doing. No offense, but you look like you put your lipstick on while trying to bust a bronc."

With a screech, Kate hurried off to the restroom. Based on the mess she had to clean up, Jared figured he and Tommy would have time for a nice visit.

After Kate disappeared, Jared shifted his attention to Tommy. "Are you Billy Joe Tate's brother?"

Tommy had been looking at the door to the girls' room, but now he glanced at Jared. "Yeah. He's one of my brothers. What are you going to do to Kate? You can't tell her dad. He'll ground her for like a million years. Maybe more."

This was priceless. Billy Joe Tate's brother defending Gavin Monroe's daughter. Growing up, Billy Joe had spent the better part of his high school years tormenting Gavin.

Yep, this was too ironic for words.

"What do you think I should do about you and Kate?"

Tommy asked hopefully, "Is letting us off the hook one of my choices?"

Jared could no longer stop himself from laughing. Tommy was priceless. "You're kidding, right?"

"But nothing happened. We were just kissing, you know? That's all."

At that moment, Jared felt older than dirt. Not too long ago, teachers were finding him in that very same closet kissing girls.

"I'll have to think about it," he finally told Tommy. "But while I'm thinking, you and Kate cool it. Deal?"

Tommy shifted his weight from one battered sneaker to the other. "I guess, but that's going to be hard. Kate is such a great kisser and I—"

"Whoa, whoa." Jared held up one hand. "Too much information. A simple 'Yes, Jared' is enough."

"Enough what?"

At the sound of Leigh's voice, Jared slowly turned. She stood at the top of the stairs and looked none too happy.

"Enough?" She arched one eyebrow and tapped one foot. Yep, she was one unhappy camper, or in this case, one unhappy homecoming coordinator.

Jared asked, "Enough what what?"

She groaned. "Don't play dumb."

"Want me to play smart instead?" he teased.

Leigh rolled her eyes and snorted. "That'll be the day."

Jared chuckled. "I'm so glad we're friends. You're so kind to my ego."

He could practically feel frustration oozing off Leigh, but he didn't want to tell her about Tommy and Kate. Not right away. After giving it some thought, he'd decided to give the kids a break.

"From what I can see, your ego is in great shape." She looked at the flip chart in Tommy's hands. "Anyone want to explain to me why it's so difficult to bring that downstairs? Half the town is in the gym, waiting for that chart so we can start planning the parade." She gave both Tommy and Jared a narrow-eyed look. "Do you know what it takes to entertain that many residents of Honey?"

Jared nodded toward the chart. "We're all set."

Leigh looked thoroughly exasperated. "Good. I was starting to think this hallway was the Bermuda Triangle. People keep coming up here and then never come back downstairs. Now let's go."

She took a couple of steps, then stopped. "Wait a minute. Where's Kate?"

Tommy blushed and looked at Jared. In turn, Jared looked at Leigh, who repeated, "Where's Kate?"

At that moment, Kate came out of the girls' room. She looked slightly better, but not enough that Leigh didn't immediately know what had happened.

"You've got to be kidding me." She stared at Tommy. "You two were making out up here?"

"Ms. Barrett, it's not like we planned it or anything," Tommy said. "We were in the closet, getting the stuff you asked for, and Kate said she thought I'd rocked in last week's game." He shrugged. "Next thing I knew, we were kissing."

Kate bobbed her head. "That's right. Tommy and I have never even talked to each other before you sent us to that closet."

Oh, now this was too good to let slide. Jared couldn't resist saying, "So, Leigh, when you think about it, if you hadn't sent them to that closet, they wouldn't have started talking. And if they hadn't started talking, well, then they certainly wouldn't have started kissing." Leigh glared at him, but he couldn't help adding, "So when you think about it, this is really your fault."

With a groan, Leigh turned and headed down the stairs. "This is so unbelievable," she said as they all made their way back to the gym. "As if I don't have enough aggravation in my life what with my family and this homecoming thing and Jared, you two end up making out in the closet. Jeez. What's next? A tornado? Or how about a swarm of locusts? We've never had one of those in Honey, but hey, the way my life is going, I'm sure there's one just around the corner waiting to pay us a visit."

They'd reached the bottom of the stairs. Leigh stopped and faced them. "I don't want anything like this happening ever again."

As Jared watched, quite a few of the parade committee members wandered out of the gym and stood directly behind Leigh. Apparently, they were wondering what the ruckus was, but Leigh was too wound up to hear them. Instead, she was busy glaring at him, Tommy, and Kate.

Figuring he'd better warn her that she had an audience, Jared said, "Um, Leigh, there's a crowd—"

But Leigh cut him off. "I'm trying to land a job here, and you people aren't helping. So from now on, I want everybody to keep their body parts to themselves. Got it?"

A gasp ran through the crowd, and Jared laughed. Well, Leigh was right about one thing. It sure was going to be a long night.

Leigh turned slowly, hoping she'd been wrong. She had to be wrong. No one was standing behind her. They couldn't be.

But true to the way her life was going these days,

not only were there people behind her, but there were lots and lots of people behind her.

Great. Just great.

She forced a smile on her face. "Hi. I guess we're ready to start."

Mary Monroe, Gavin's mother and Kate's grandmother, stepped forward. "What were you talking about a second ago?"

Silently, Leigh sighed. Okeydokey. There went her career, up in flames. "You see, there was—"

Jared stepped forward. "Leigh's upset because rather than hurrying with the flip chart, Tommy and I got talking about football. I was showing him a play we made during the homecoming game in '88, and I almost ended up shoving them all down the stairs."

Leigh stared at him. Didn't he realize he was giving this town one more reason to think badly of him? She looked at him and shook her head slightly. He didn't need to throw himself on this grenade.

But he only grinned and winked. Then he walked over to Mary Monroe, and said, "I'm sorry. I'll have to be more careful next time. But at least Kate wasn't hurt."

The older woman frowned. "You're still as wild as you were growing up."

With a huff, she headed back toward the gym with Kate in tow. The rest of the town eventually followed, and Jared would have, too, but Leigh stopped him.

No matter how long she tried, she would never be able to figure out Jared Kendrick. He was trying so hard to get the town to forget his past, and then he'd just voluntarily given these people yet another reason to say bad things about him.

"I don't get you," she admitted.

Jared chuckled. "Is this where I'm supposed to say you could get me if you tried?"

"Hardeharhar." Moving closer, she poked him with one finger. "You know what I mean. Why did you tell Mary you'd almost knocked her precious Kate down the stairs? You know she's going to tell every single person who comes into the drugstore how irresponsible you are. That can really hurt your rodeo school."

Apparently, he wasn't too thrilled with her poking him in the chest, because he wrapped one hand around hers. "For starters, ouch."

"Oh, pulleese. You're a big, bad rodeo rider. I'm not hurting you."

His grin was sexy as all get out, and as usual, it made Leigh's heart race.

"Maybe I'm more sensitive than you think," he told her with a twinkle in his amazing brown eyes. "Maybe I'm easily hurt."

"Ha. That will be the day. You've had horses toss you a bunch of times. You're big and strong and tough."

He lightly stroked her hand, which he still held against his chest. "Oops. Watch yourself there, Leigh. You came awfully close to complimenting me."

Maybe she had. She hadn't really intended on doing anything but chewing him out for not backing her up when she'd been lecturing Kate and Tommy.

But now that she thought about it, maybe his approach was the right one. He'd gone out of his way to make sure those kids weren't humiliated in front of the citizens of Honey.

"Maybe you deserve the compliment. This time. That was a good thing you did for Tommy and Kate tonight," she admitted.

His grin grew wider. "Mary Monroe hasn't liked me since I bought a box of condoms in her store the day I turned eighteen. Unlike Kate and Tommy, I had nothing to lose."

She playfully shoved at his shoulder. "How am I supposed to stay mad at you if you do nice things?"

He grinned that slow, sexy grin of his that made her tingle all over with awareness. She loved it when he grinned like that. She also hated it. That grin really got to her.

"Maybe you'll just have to stop being mad at me,"

he said. "We're friends, now. We should work harder at getting along."

Friends. That was right. They were friends.

She took a step backward, away from all the temptation she felt whenever she was near Jared.

"Thank you for being nice to Tommy and Kate," she finally managed to say.

"Do you realize you gave me both a please and a thank you tonight? I'm on a roll."

"Let's hope so. Let's hope your noble deed doesn't end up hurting your new business," Leigh said.

With one last slow caress, he released her hand and opened the door to the gym for her. "The funny thing is I seem to be attracting customers because of my wild reputation."

Leigh stared at him. "Let me guess. These customers are all female."

"Seems like you're not the only lady in town who'd like to find out what sort of talents I have," he said dryly. "Like I told you on Monday, that's exactly why I need your help figuring out which women in this town are interested in a serious relationship, not just a quick roll in the hay."

Leigh frowned. Women were signing up at his school in the hopes of seducing him? Boy, that stunk. She taught school during the week and was busy on the weekends. She couldn't sign up for classes. Not that she wanted to. Um...

She was getting another of those headaches she only got when she was around him. "Let's get this meeting over with."

Jared nodded. "Good idea. And who knows? Maybe you'll notice someone at the meeting tonight who's perfect for me. What do you think?"

His comment felt like ice dropped down her shirt. "I know someone who might like to go out with you," she said, biting back a smile. "In fact, she's here tonight. In Mr. Buckingham's classroom."

Jared looked confused. "In the classroom? I thought all the teachers had left for the night." Although she knew it wasn't fair, Leigh was enjoying this little game. "They have. But Connie Pearl Reardon always stays here. She's very loyal."

"Is she on the cleaning crew?" he asked.

Leigh shook her head. "No."

With a sigh, Jared said, "I'm lost, then. Why is this woman here? For the meeting?"

With effort, Leigh held in a laugh. "No. She's not coming to the meeting. But now that you mention it, she might be interested in joining the parade."

"Leigh, dang it, what are you talking about? Who is this woman?"

She couldn't help herself anymore. She laughed. "Connie Pearl Reardon happens to be a dummy."

"Seems to me you had some trouble with algebra in the ninth grade," Jared pointed out.

Leigh laughed again, her good mood rapidly returning. "No, you don't understand. She's a real dummy. You know, the kind they use to teach CPR."

With a groan, Jared said, "I get it. Connie Pearl Reardon—CPR. So the only female in the whole place you think will go out with me is a rubber dummy in health class? Man, I must be losing my touch."

No, that wasn't the only female she thought would go out with him...as he well knew. "I think you're missing out on a golden opportunity with Connie Pearl. She's quiet and polite and definitely wants to settle down. In fact, she's the type of woman who stays where you put her."

"No offense to Connie Pearl," he said slowly, "but I prefer my women a lot more animated." The sexy way he said the word animated made the air in Leigh's lungs sort of whoosh out. She stared at him for a second, and then with effort, slammed her brain back in gear.

"I'll make a mental note," she said dryly. "And store it someplace safe in my brain."

Jared chuckled and fell into step next to her as

they crossed the gym. "You know, sometimes I get the feeling you're not really intending on helping me find my soulmate."

Gee, now how'd he figure that one out?

"I think you're capable of trolling for your own dates," she told him. "But if you really want me to keep trying, I will."

Thankfully, they'd reached the center of the gym. Anxious to get the meeting going, Leigh sat in the first empty chair she found and said, "Who has the list of parade entrants?"

Tommy brought it over and gave it to her. She didn't miss that he no longer looked her in the eye.

Too bad. The kid had a bright future. This was his senior year, and because of his football skill and good grades, it looked like he was going to get offered a lot of scholarships to some very impressive colleges. But if he got involved with the daughter of the principal, there was no telling what might happen to those scholarships.

"Thanks, Tommy." Leigh studied the list and immediately saw some serious problems. When someone dragged out the chair next to her and sat, she didn't even bother to see who it was. She knew it was Jared.

Refusing to let him distract her yet again, she

looked at the crowd and shook her head. "Nope. This order for the parade isn't going to work."

"But we like it," said Patty. "We took a vote while you people were off doing whatever it was you did."

Leigh resisted the temptation to roll her eyes. Instead, she forced herself to say calmly, "No offense, but you've got the horses leading the parade."

Bud stepped forward. "That's right. We figure since it's Wild Westival, we should start the parade off with a Western theme."

She could hear the muted sound of Jared's chuckle.

"No offense, Leigh," Mary said, "but if you're going to wander off during the meeting, you really shouldn't criticize the plans we develop."

Hey, she had not wandered off. She'd gone to find out what had happened to Tommy and Kate and Jared. If anything, she'd been on a rescue mission.

"I don't think she's criticizing," Jared said. "Just pointing out an obvious fact."

Leigh appreciated his support. "That's right. If the horses go first, the rest of the parade will have a lot of dodging to do."

Steve Myerson leaned forward. According to the list, he planned on walking in the parade, towing his lazy dog Rufus in a wagon.

Sheesh.

"Isn't there some way we can teach the horses not to do that?" Steve asked. "Then there wouldn't be a problem."

This time, Leigh was the one who bit back a laugh. "Yeah, Kendrick. Just tell your horses to wait until they get home."

Jared looked at Steve and said, "Sorry. These horses aren't housebroken."

The committee members did a lot of moaning and groaning, but eventually, once the band teacher, Annie Croft, said there was no way she and the marching band were following horses, the rest of the group went along with the change in plans.

Over the next hour, they negotiated then counter-negotiated, then counter-counter-negotiated the order in which everyone would be in the parade. Finally, most people seemed happy until Annie Croft said, "I still think the band should go near the end rather than right at the beginning of the parade."

"The music might startle the horses," Jared pointed out.

"Couldn't we work with them to get them used to it? I'd like the band to be the grand finale," she persisted.

Leigh shook her head. "Annie, it's too risky."

"But think how exciting the finale would be if we

could teach the horses to do tricks." Annie waved one hand. "It would be a triumph."

Jared looked confused as he said, "These horses have been trained to do barrel racing, and I have some cutting horses that can—"

Annie shook her head. "No, no. What I want to know is, can they dance?"

Jared made a choking sound. "You want my horses to dance?"

Annie nodded. "A little. If they can. You know, maybe sway side-to-side. See, the band is considering playing the 'Hokey Pokey,' and I thought it would be cute if the horses followed us and danced to the song."

Leigh was unable to stop her mouth from dropping open, but at least no one noticed her, because Jared burst out laughing. Really long. And hard.

At first, Leigh figured Annie was kidding. But the expression on the woman's face made it clear she was perfectly serious.

She truly wanted Jared's horses to dance the "Hokey Pokey."

Looked like they still had a lot of negotiating left to do tonight.

5

"Thanks a lot for changing your mind," Steve said, pumping Jared's hand. "I know my brother's family is going to have a great time here."

Jared scuffed the ground with one boot heel. Glad to know someone was going to enjoy themselves because he sure as shooting wasn't going to. He'd just agreed to host Steve's brother and his family for a week. No, host was the wrong word. He was going to entertain them, like some kind of six-foot-tall amusement park.

Now, not only did his students mostly consist of women who were more interested in coming on to him than in learning how to barrel race. They also consisted of dude ranchers, people who wanted to spend a week on a ranch so they could play cowboy.

Looking downright gleeful, Steve climbed back into his purple minivan. "I really appreciate this, Jared. My brother is tickled pink." Then, with a wide grin, he added, "And I don't care what anyone says about you, you're one heck of a guy." With that as his final comment, Steve honked his horn, waved frantically out of the window, and drove away like a big grape rolling down the driveway.

"Dang," Jared muttered. "You're one sorry excuse for a businessman." After Steve had disappeared, Jared headed up the porch steps to his house. This rodeo school was turning out to be just about everything else but a rodeo school. So far, his school was a combination dude ranch and ladies' club.

He dropped into one of the rocking chairs on his porch. But what choice did he have? Setting up a rodeo school took money. Lots of money. Money he didn't have.

He'd hoped students would sign up, and he could reinvest their tuitions into upgrading the school. Unfortunately, he'd discovered there were two types of rodeo school customers: the ones with money, who immediately signed up with the established schools, and the ones without two dimes, who immediately gravitated to him.

He already had two guys, Stan and Dwayne, who

were helping out in exchange for lessons. He didn't need any more down-and-out students.

He needed students with money. So at least for now, he'd work with the local ladies, even if they had about as much interest in learning to rope and ride as they did in splitting the atom. And he'd let Steve's brother and his brood stay at the ranch, because at this point, money was money.

Leaning back in his chair, he watched a truck pull in his driveway. The way his luck was going, this was probably some local dad wanting to know if Jared did pony rides for children's birthday parties.

But thankfully, once the truck got closer, he saw it was Chase Barrett. Good. Chase might not be a prospective student, but he also wasn't about to ask Jared to teach him to "ride the pretty horsies." No, if he had to guess, Jared would wager Chase was here on an official big brother mission. The Barrett brothers were probably hearing all sorts of things about him and Leigh. Knowing those three, they'd want some strong reassurance that his intentions toward their baby sister were honorable.

No problem there. His intentions were honorable. Leigh's, however, weren't.

"Hey," Chase said, getting out of his truck and heading up the porch steps. "How's it going?"

"Good. What brings you here?"

Chase sat in the chair next to Jared. "This and that."

Jared nodded. "Which you want to talk about first, this or that?"

With a chuckle, Chase pulled off his Stetson. "Let's start with this first."

"This being Leigh, right?"

"You're one smart fellow," Chase said.

Yeah, well, it didn't exactly take a rocket scientist to figure out the direction of this conversation. "What do you want to know about Leigh?"

"For starters, mind running me through what happened at the reception? I know that dance floor was mighty crowded, and people got kinda squashed, but you and Leigh were the only ones who had trouble with their clothing."

"Noticed that, did you?"

"Most of the town did since when the song ended, you two had to get dressed again. Then I understand things got kinda chummy with you and Leigh at the cafe a few nights ago."

When Chase took a breath, Jared added, "Plus things got a little dicey at the parade planning meeting."

Chase nodded. "That's what folks are saying."

"So what do all those 'folks' think is going on? Do

they think I'm trying to seduce Leigh and lead her astray?"

"I believe that's the popular theory."

Man, this was amazing, but unfortunately, not very surprising. "Have any of these people actually met your sister? Do they honestly believe anyone could lead Leigh anywhere?"

Chase laughed. "Yeah, I see what you mean. She's always been a tough one."

"If you know Leigh's not about to let anyone do anything she doesn't want, why are you here, Chase?"

He shrugged. "I'm her brother, and I love her. I'd be falling down on my brotherly duties if I didn't at least ask why you unzipped her dress at the wedding reception."

"I unzipped her dress because she unbuttoned my vest." Before Chase could say anything, he went on. "You should know that Leigh unbuttoned my vest first. And not because she was overcome with lust. She was mad at me."

"And why is that?"

Jared debated for a second just how honest to be with Chase. Finally, he decided he might as well put his cards on the table. "Last summer when Leigh went out with me, she only did it because she wanted to drive you and your brothers crazy," he confessed.

Chase didn't seem surprised. "Yep, that's my

sister. Born to drive her kin insane." He tipped his head and looked at Jared. "But see, what I can't understand is why she's mad at you. Seems natural to me you'd be irked at her, but she's got nothing to be upset about."

With a shrug, Jared explained, "I didn't go along with her plan."

Chase chuckled. "Okay. Now I get it. She had you pegged as some easy fun, right? But you refused to cooperate. That sure would fry Leigh's bacon. When she makes a plan, she doesn't like it foiled."

"So she's explained to me in her own special way," Jared said dryly.

"What happens now?"

"Nothing. Leigh and I have decided to be friends." Even saying the word made him crazy, but he knew he had to take things slowly. But before he was through, he was going to move heaven and earth to make sure they became a lot more than friends to each other.

For the moment, though, he'd bide his time. If he rushed her, Leigh would figure out what he was up to and never speak to him again.

"You know, Megan and I started out as friends," Chase pointed out. "Now we're happily married with a ba—" He abruptly stopped talking.

Jared turned to look at Chase. He knew why the

other man had stopped talking, but he couldn't help teasing. "You and Megan have a ba? What kind of ba? Where'd you get it? In Dallas? I hear they have the best 'bas' around."

Chase chuckled. "Shut up. You didn't hear a blasted thing from me."

Understanding that Chase and Megan weren't ready for the news of their impending parenthood to be spread all over Honey, Jared nodded. "Gotcha. I'll keep your ba a secret until such time as everyone knows about it." He couldn't help adding, "And congratulations."

Chase grinned. "Thanks. But my point was that sometimes you start out as friends, but then you fall in love and end up being—"

"The parents of a ba."

With a chuckle, Chase agreed. "Something like that."

Jared liked to think that was a possibility, but a lot had to change before he could even think about having a family with Leigh. For starters, he had to get her to see him as more than stud material.

From what he could tell, that alone was going to take some doing.

"So, if you and Leigh did become more than friends, do you think something might come of it?"

Although Chase pretended to be casual, Jared knew he wasn't at all.

"I want to settle here and put down roots," Jared confessed. "Unfortunately, at the moment, Leigh wants to enjoy her newly found freedom. She wants to be independent and have some long-awaited fun."

"If you ask me, you're being too nice, Jared," Chase told him. "I love my sister, and I'd do anything for her, but the way she's feeling now, she may not even give you a chance if you're looking for something more long-term. Guess the boys and I kept her on too tight a rope. She's a wild one, and we never wanted to see her get hurt. Bad mistake, because now she's going to run since she's finally got some room."

"Seems that way."

Chase leaned back in his chair. "I guess we all have to let her make her own choices."

There was nothing Jared could say to that, and for a few moments, they sat in silence.

Then Chase said, "Yep. She'll make her own choices. Like tonight, for instance. She's going to that new multiplex in Tyler with some guy who works for Nathan. The guy told Emma they're going to go see that tearjerker movie. Guess that's what Leigh wants out of life. To go to see sad movies with some guy who just moved into town a week ago and who no one knows a blasted thing about. But hey, it's her choice."

Jared frowned. Leigh was going all the way to Tyler with some guy she didn't know? Some guy no one in Honey knew?

Didn't seem too wise. But all he said to Chase was, "I'm sure this guy is nice. Otherwise, Nathan wouldn't have hired him."

Chase snorted. "A person can seem real nice at work and be completely different on a date." He stood. "Another person can have the whole town convinced he's no good just because he was a little wild when he was a kid. But that man actually would be the good guy. The one a woman might not realize is the right guy for her. Not if she was too busy going out with the wrong guy. Who might act like who knows what on a date."

Jared laughed. "That's the most convoluted explanation I've ever heard. You could have hurt yourself just saying it."

Chase put his Stetson on. "Yeah, well, just for the record, you didn't hear any of it from me."

With that, Chase climbed into his truck and headed down the driveway. Jared watched him go. Man, that had been one bizarre visit. But then again, most of his encounters with the good people of Honey were strange. This town had to be too close to a toxic waste dump or something because the inhabitants were peculiar.

"Strange, strange, strange," he muttered to himself as he headed inside his house. It was almost time for dinner. He could go out to eat or maybe cook something he'd picked up at the grocery store this morning.

When he reached the kitchen, he opened the refrigerator. Nothing inside looked good. And the thought of going to Roy's Cafe in Honey didn't sound appetizing, either.

What he really felt like eating was...popcorn. A big barrel of movie popcorn.

Was he really going to drive all the way into Tyler to bust up Leigh's date with this guy? He grinned. Hell, yes. Sure, some might think he was a conniving jerk, but Leigh was the woman for him. He had to fight for her, didn't he?

Besides, going to a movie sure did sound like fun. And no one said he had to go to the one Leigh was going to see. Maybe he'd go to a completely different theater and see a completely different movie.

He walked over and grabbed his keys off the hook by the back door. "Guess I'm getting as peculiar as the rest of this town because now I'm lying to myself."

Still, that didn't stop him. He headed out the

back door and off to Tyler, figuring the worse that could happen was Leigh would hate him for the rest of his life.

But hey, at this point, he'd try anything.

"You're really quiet. Are you okay?"

"I'm fine." Leigh glanced over at her date, Travis Armstrong. They were on their way to the movies. She should be having a great time. A terrific time. Travis was a nice guy, and she was certain their date would be nothing like her last one with Billy Joe Tate.

But ever since Travis had picked her up, she hadn't been able to pay a bit of attention to anything he'd been saying. Instead, she'd been thinking about what she was always thinking about—Jared. She hadn't seen him since the parade committee meeting two days ago, and already she felt antsy. Restless.

Talk about being stupider than a rock. Why would she waste perfectly good time thinking about Jared? There were so many other interesting and important things she could think about. Like...well, if she thought long enough, she was sure she could come up with a few.

Focusing her attention on Travis, she asked, "What movie do you want to see?"

Travis parked his car in the crowded movie parking lot. He'd driven them all the way to Tyler since Honey didn't have a movie theater. But Tyler had several multiplexes, and Travis had picked the biggest of the bunch.

"I figured you'd like to see *Buckets of Tears*," he said. "So that's what we're going to see."

He had to be kidding? She wasn't the three-hanky kind at all. Resisting the impulse to make a gagging noise, she said subtly, "That's sweet of you, Travis, but why don't we see *Spies and Lies* or maybe that campus comedy, *Idiot U* instead? They both look good."

Travis shook his head. "Ah, Leigh, that's nice of you, but Bree always said...I mean, I know ladies like sad movies."

"Who's Bree?"

Leigh watched with fascination as a bright-red blush colored Travis' round face.

"She and I used to date," he finally said with a shrug.

Since Leigh knew practically everyone in Honey, and she didn't know Bree, this woman had to be someone Travis knew from before. "How long did you date her?"

"A while."

Uh-oh. That didn't sound good. "What's a while?"

Travis sighed long and loud. "We met when we first started school."

"When you were freshmen?"

When he shook his head, suspicion crept up Leigh's spine.

"Before that. Let's just forget Bree and enjoy this movie."

Leigh put one hand on his arm. "No way. Tell me when you first met Bree."

It took a lot of moaning and groaning, but finally Travis blurted, "In kindergarten. We met in kindergarten."

Leigh's mouth dropped open. "You're kidding? But you didn't start liking each other until much later, right? Maybe until you met again in college." This time when Travis sighed, Leigh was the one who groaned. "You're seriously telling me you were together with Bree from kindergarten on? When did you break up?"

"Recently," was all Travis said, but the way he said it in such a gloomy voice pretty much spoke volumes.

Uh-oh. That didn't sound good. "Until how recently?"

"Um, you know when I moved to town last week to go to work for your brother Nathan?"

Ah, jeez, she could see where this was going.

"Travis, are you telling me you just broke up with your girlfriend of twenty years last week?"

He hung his head. "She broke up with me. She didn't want to move to Honey, but I wanted this job."

This was much, much worse than her date with Billy Joe Tate. At least Billy had only been hung up on his car.

"You're still in love with Bree, aren't you?" Leigh asked, knowing full well that this date was going to be a dud before it even started.

"I thought if I went out on a date, I might feel better. I know it's very important to get on with my life." Travis sighed again. "I'll admit, dating someone else actually feels kind of...bizarre. But I'm sure I'll get over that feeling."

Bizarre? Going out with her felt bizarre? Now wasn't that romantic? What was wrong with the men in this town? What did it take for a reasonably attractive woman to have a little fun?

She looked at Travis, who had a sad, puppy-dog expression on his face. Drat, drat, drat. She could tell he wanted to pour his heart out about his ex-girlfriend. Somehow, she'd become a shoulder to cry on rather than an object of lust.

Ah, for crying out loud. She wanted some fun. Some wildness. She'd gotten her blasted brothers married off. This was supposed to be the time of her life.

But she couldn't just ignore Travis, so she said, "Tell you what, let's go see something funny. Maybe that will cheer you up."

"You're so nice," he said. "But really, I want to see what you want to see." He pushed open his door. "Let's hurry. We don't want to be late to *Buckets of Tears*."

As far as she was concerned, late was the only way to arrive at that movie. She'd rather tie her own arms into a pretzel knot than spend almost three hours watching that film.

But Travis seemed adamant, so rather than upset him, Leigh decided she could use the time to nap. "Fine. Let's see the sad movie."

Secretly, she hoped the film might be sold out when they got to the ticket booth, but no such luck. It was a Friday night and most everything was sold out. Not only were there no seats left for the two movies she'd suggested, there were also no seats left in the next showing of the kid's movie with a talking alligator, the ninja movie, the good cop/bad cop movie and the two foreign films. The choice became either wait around for over an hour for one of the other movies to start...or go to *Buckets of Tears*.

"Come on. It won't be so bad," Travis said, buying the tickets.

Yeah, right, and waxing your legs didn't hurt. She just knew this movie was going to be right up there with having a root canal on the enjoyment scale.

But she didn't want to hurt Travis' feelings. He was already so upset that she felt the least she could do was pretend to have a good time. Plus, she wasn't about to let another of her dates end before it really started. A woman could only take so much.

After getting a big tub of popcorn, they entered the theater. Surprisingly, a lot of people were there, although Leigh didn't miss that most of the patrons were women.

"Where would you like to sit?" she asked, still hoping he'd suggest they sit in the next theater.

"Anyplace is good." Travis glanced around. "Hey, look over there. A crowd has formed. Someone sure is popular."

Leigh leaned around Travis a little and studied the group. Five or six women stood clumped around one seat, all of them chattering loudly and laughing.

"Must be one of their friends," she said, glancing toward the back of the theater. Napping would be easier if she was away from a crowd. "Why don't we sit near the top?"

With a shrug, Travis started up the stairs. They'd

only taken a couple of steps when a loud giggle made Leigh turn toward the group of women again. The one giggling moved a fraction of an inch, and Leigh caught a glimpse of the person sitting in the seat.

Jared. Jared was sitting in the middle of the theater being fawned and fussed over by all those women.

"That rat," she muttered. "That absolute rat."

"Who's a rat?" Travis followed her gaze. "Look, there's Jared. Let's go sit by him."

"You know Jared?"

"Not personally. But I read about his rodeo school in the *Honey Times*. I know a lot of the people in town talk about him, but he seems like a great guy."

Oh, no, Jared was most certainly not a great guy. A great guy wouldn't follow you around and drive you crazy. A great guy wouldn't ask you to be friends and find him dates. Most importantly, a great guy would have sex with a lady when she asked him to.

Whatever else Jared was, he wasn't a great guy.

"I'd rather sit higher up," Leigh said, hoping against hope they could find seats before Jared noticed them. Unfortunately, good luck had deserted her long ago, because just as she tugged on Travis' arm, Jared turned his head and caught sight of them.

Dang it all.

A slow, sexy smile crossed his face, and then he

said something to the women because they eventually wandered off.

"Hey, Leigh. I didn't know you were coming to this movie," Jared said.

Before she could do a thing to stop him, Travis headed over to introduce himself to Jared, and then plopped down in the seat next to him. Oh, wasn't this just peachy. First Jared had ruined her date with Billy Joe, and now he was butting into her date with Travis.

Reluctantly, she came over to where the men were sitting. "What are you doing here?" she asked Jared.

He grinned, but she didn't miss for a second the sparkle in his eyes. "I was planning on watching a movie. Isn't that what most of the people are doing here?"

"This can't possibly be a coincidence. Not this time. Stop following me," she said.

Travis looked at her, obviously confused. "How can he be following you if he was here first?"

Leigh opened her mouth to respond, and then realized she didn't have an answer to that. She might have conceded the point, but Jared looked way too pleased with himself for her to believe this wasn't planned.

"Trust me, I'm not following you," Jared said, although he looked like he was going to laugh at any second. "Why would I do something like that?"

She didn't know why he was doing it; she just knew he was. She was prepared to keep discussing this, but the lights dimmed, and the previews started.

"Leigh, come on and sit," Travis said. "You don't want to miss the movie. Should be good."

Suddenly, delightfully, a thought occurred to Leigh. If Jared had followed her, then he was going to have to sit through this tear-fest. She could hardly wait to watch him squirm and sigh for the next almost three hours of tragedy.

Biting back a smile, she sat next to Travis. This movie would teach Jared to stop butting into her dates.

And during the next hour, she realized this movie was indeed torture. The heroine lost her family in a flood, her best friends in a fire, her fiancé in an earthquake, and now her beloved poodle looked like he was about to be history based on the smoke puffing out of the volcano in the background.

Around her, Leigh could hear the sad sniffles of many of the other patrons. Once or twice, she'd even heard a soft sniff from Travis.

But Leigh had spent most of the time wondering why the heroine didn't get off her duff and prevent these problems. She was without a doubt dumber than mud, and Leigh's eyes hurt from rolling them so much.

When the poodle started running up the hill straight toward the lava while the dimwitted heroine talked on her cell phone, Leigh decided she'd had enough.

"I'm going for a soda," she told Travis. "Do you want anything?"

"No," Travis said vaguely, obviously engrossed in the film.

Right as Leigh stood, Jared said, "I'd like a popcorn. I think I'll come with you."

As if.

"That's okay, I'll get it for you," she told him, then she sprinted toward the lobby before he could argue. She didn't want to have to talk to Jared because if she did, she knew it would end in a fight.

No, she'd simply get Jared's popcorn. And since she didn't know how he liked it, she'd be sure to tell the kid behind the counter to drench it in butter.

It was a silly, juvenile gesture, sure, but it was the best she could come up with at the moment.

After getting a soda and Jared's popcorn, she headed back toward the theater. Partway back to her seat, she literally ran into Travis.

"Hi," she said. "Where are you off to?"

She couldn't make out his expression in the darkened theater, but she clearly heard him sigh.

"I think you're terrific, really. But I can't do this. I

realize that Bree is the woman for me. I love her, and I'm going to go call her." He patted her arm. "Jared said he'd give you a ride home. Thanks for understanding, Leigh."

Then he walked away.

Leigh blinked. Hello? Who said she understood? She most definitely didn't understand.

She narrowed her eyes and glanced toward the middle of the theater. Jared. She knew he'd had something to do with Travis' sudden decision to rush home and call Bree.

Determined, she headed over to Jared and slipped into the seat Travis had vacated. Even in the faint light, she could tell Jared had his eyes closed. He wasn't watching the movie; he was dozing.

"You're a rat. No, you're worse than a rat. You're whatever rats hate," she practically hissed at him, not wanting to ruin the movie for the rest of the audience but unable to wait another second to tell him what she thought of his plotting.

He opened his eyes and grinned. "I love it when you whisper sweet nothings to me."

Leigh snorted. "As if."

Jared chuckled. "Seriously, I'm sorry Travis left. The second you walked away, he started talking about his ex-fiancée and how much he missed her. All I said was 'hmmmm.'"

"Why are you doing this to me?" she asked. "You turned me down, so stop ruining my dates. You keep saying we're friends. Why don't you act like one for a change?"

A woman behind them said loudly, "Shhh."

Jared leaned close to Leigh and whispered, "I didn't set out to ruin your date. I didn't do anything."

Leigh sincerely doubted that, although realistically, Travis hadn't seemed in the mood for this date. He should have never asked her out since he was in love with another woman.

Still, all that didn't mean Jared wasn't guilty. Of something.

"I can't figure out why you're doing this," she said as much to herself as to him.

Again, the woman behind them said, "Shhh."

Leigh glanced at the screen. The poodle, which as far as she could tell was the smartest thing in the movie, was running away from the lava. But the dumb heroine's heel had gotten stuck, and now she was crying as the lava approached.

Boy, this was one stupid movie.

Jared must have agreed, because he snagged her hand and stood. "Come on. Let's get out of here. I can't take this anymore."

Finally, there was something they agreed on. She

shoved the box of popcorn at him, grabbed her soda and purse, and went with him.

"This is the worst movie I've ever seen," she muttered as they headed toward the exit. "And for the record, no woman in real life is as dumb as that heroine."

They'd reached the lobby, and she turned to face him. "I'm not as dumb as that heroine. I know you're up to something. I know it as sure as I know my shoe size."

She took a couple of steps closer and gave him a narrow-eyed look. "I don't know what it is yet, but I'll figure it out. Trust me. I'll figure it out."

6

He hadn't set out to ruin her date. He really hadn't. But he knew he had about as much chance of convincing her of that as he had of teaching his horses to knit. All he'd wanted to do was remind Leigh that he was around.

It wasn't his fault her dates were losers. How was he supposed to know that the second Leigh walked away, Travis would go on and on about some woman he'd once planned on marrying? And then, with absolutely no encouragement, the guy had decided to go call this love of his life.

Leaving a fit-to-be-tied Leigh behind.

Leigh tossed her soda cup in the trash and headed toward the exit. "Okay, you've ruined my date. Again. Let's go home."

She was out the door and a good way across the

parking lot before he knew what was happening. When he caught up with her, he pointed out, "Technically, I didn't ruin your date. Your date ruined your date. Travis was the one who decided to leave. I don't think he even planned on telling you he was going. I think he was going to sneak out. If you ask me, that was a crummy thing to do. He should have at least offered to drive you home."

Leigh looked at him. "That would have been better? He could have said, 'Thanks for the wonderful date. I had a great time. I'd call you again, but being with you has convinced me I'm in love with another woman.' Jeez, talk about flattering."

Yeah, she had a point there.

"Well, don't take it personally," Jared told her, turning her in the direction of his truck. "Travis was one confused guy. It sounds like he never should have broken up with this woman in the first place."

Leigh sighed. "I guess you're right. But I seem to have the worst luck when it comes to picking dates. And I'm not doing such a hot job picking friends, either."

Jared laughed. "Hey!"

She put her hands on her hips. "Seriously, you're not helping any by showing up."

"Fine. Here's an idea. Why don't I help you pick better dates, and then I won't have to show up?"

Leigh frowned. "What?"

"Let me pick your next date. And I promise, I won't ruin it."

He could tell Leigh was debating with herself, so he upped his offer. "It's only fair since I'm letting you pick my next date. And remember, we already agreed —no senior citizens, okay?"

For a second, he thought she'd tell him no way, but suddenly, she relented. "Fine. I guess it can't be any worse that what I've been picking on my own."

They'd reached his new black truck, and he unlocked the passenger door and held it open for her.

"Where's your motor scooter?" she asked as she climbed in the truck. "Amanda said you drove a motor scooter."

"Ha, ha. My motorcycle is home. I decided to drive my truck instead."

She studied the truck slowly. "You know, this looks like the Batmobile."

"Hardeharhar," he said, using one of her favorite lines. After she got in, he closed her door and walked around to the driver's side. Okay, so maybe his truck was a little on the seriously black side, but it was hardly the Batmobile.

When he opened his door, Leigh asked, "What do all these buttons on the ceiling do?"

"Well, the one you're pushing opens my garage door," he said dryly.

"Oooh. The entrance to the Batcave. Got it." Jared climbed in and tossed his leather jacket on the seat between them. "It's just a truck, Leigh."

She rolled her eyes. "Excuse me. Have you looked at this thing? It has more gizmos and gadgets than the space shuttle."

He chuckled and started the engine. "You're easily impressed."

She gave him a look that spoke volumes. "Hardly."

"Okay. So if this is the Batmobile, does that make you Catwoman? 'Cause if you're interested in putting on that skintight black outfit, I'm on board with the whole concept."

Leigh snorted. "Dream on."

Yeah, no doubt he would tonight.

"I like this truck," he said, turning on the CD player and heading back to Honey. "I needed a truck because of the rodeo school, but I also wanted something comfortable. So I bought this."

Of course, that had been in the days when he'd been making good money. Still, he liked his truck and planned on keeping it. "I think it's practical, and yet, decadent."

She laughed. "Yes, that's you all right."

He loved the sound of her laughter. So beautiful. So sexy. So free.

"I'm not sure whether that's a compliment or an insult," he said.

"Oh, you're sure all right. You always are, Jared."

Yeah, he usually was sure of himself. But Leigh confused the hell out of him. He knew what he wanted. What he wanted her to feel for him. What he wanted them to be together.

But for the first time in his life, he was unsure how to get what he wanted. Sure, his plan seemed to be working so far, but it was like walking through a minefield. One wrong step and kapow! That would be that.

For the rest of the drive, he and Leigh discussed the parade. Despite a bumpy start, things were coming along.

"Thanks for letting us use your barn to keep the floats in," Leigh said.

"No problem. I'm sure my horses will find it entertaining. And it will give them a break from trying to learn to dance."

"Any luck with that whole 'Hokey Pokey' thing? Are they taking to it?" she asked with a giggle.

"Oddly enough, no." They reached Honey, so he headed toward Leigh's house. "And they didn't like the whole potty-training idea, either. Sorry."

Leigh giggled again. "Oh well. At least you tried."

He slowly turned his truck into the driveway of Leigh's house, very reluctant to see the evening end. After shutting off the engine, he glanced at her and felt compelled to say, "I want you to know, I didn't mean to ruin your date. It just happened."

She pushed open her door, and light flooded the cab of the truck. For a second, she just looked at him. Then she leaned over and kissed him. Hard.

This was the very last thing he'd expected her to do. But never one to miss an opportunity or to question his good luck, Jared wrapped his arms around Leigh and kissed her back.

Who cared why she'd kissed him? He sure didn't, especially when she lightly brushed the tip of her tongue across his lips.

Yeow.

Jared spent a long, long time kissing Leigh, and when she finally pulled away from him, he grinned. Man, that had been one hell of a kiss.

"Why'd you kiss me?" he couldn't help asking.

Leigh batted her eyelashes. "Why, gee whiz, I didn't mean to kiss you. It just happened."

Even though she was pretending to be unaffected by the kiss, her voice was warm and raspy. She was every bit as turned on as he was.

Good.

With a flirty wave, she hopped out of his truck and headed toward her house. When she reached the porch, she glanced over her shoulder and said, "Oh, and be careful with that popcorn in your new truck."

Then she unlocked her door and went inside.

For a second, he just looked at the closed door. Then he studied the box of popcorn next to him on the seat. The bottom was gooey. Thankfully, it hadn't hurt the upholstery. But his bomber jacket would never be the same.

Neither would he after that kiss.

"I think you're missing a golden opportunity," Leigh's sister-in-law Megan said as she took the rolls out of the oven. "If you like Jared, you should let him know."

"I don't like Jared. Not in the way you mean."

Emma laughed. "Please. I saw the way you acted around him the last time he was in town. You more than like him." She grinned at Erin and Megan. "Do you think there will be another wedding soon?"

Leigh snorted. "As if."

These women were demented. Leigh wouldn't have come to dinner with her family tonight if she'd known they were going to act this way.

Not that they ever behaved themselves. This was the Barrett clan. Even the ladies who were Barretts by marriage seemed to be developing ornery streaks.

Erin still had a golden-peachy tan from her honeymoon, so Leigh wasn't a bit surprised when she said, "You can't stop love."

Leigh groaned. "From this moment on, no more talk about love and marriage, or I'm leaving, got it?"

All three of her sisters-in-law looked at her for a moment. Then they smiled. Sweet, smug, annoying-as-all-get-out smiles.

"Fine," Megan said. "We won't discuss love or marriage."

"Can we still talk about Jared?" Emma asked. "I mean, you keep telling us you have no intention of falling in love with him, and you'll never want to marry him, right? So it's still okay to talk about him, isn't it?"

Before Leigh could answer, Trent, the youngest Barrett brother and Erin's husband, entered the kitchen. "What are you ladies talking about?"

"We're not talking about love or marriage," Erin told Trent, leaning up and kissing him. "And we're not sure yet whether we can talk about Jared, either."

Trent grinned. "I'm lost. I haven't a clue what you're talking about, or rather not talking about, but

Chase wanted me to let you know the steaks will be ready in a couple of minutes."

On his way out the door to the patio, he grabbed one of the rolls in the bowl near Leigh. "Oh, even if it's not okay to talk about Jared, I sure hope it's okay to talk to him since he's joining us for dinner."

Leigh shook her head. She'd planned for this possibility. Since Sunday dinner with her family was a tradition, she knew there was a chance Jared would try to crash it. So she'd made certain he would be busy. "No. No, he isn't. I made certain he couldn't come."

Megan moved forward and gave her a questioning look. "How?"

"He has a date tonight."

Now Emma walked over to stand by her. "How do you know that?"

"Because I set it up. I'm helping Jared find dates."

Trent laughed. "Well, you're not doing a very good job, because the lady you set him up with called this afternoon and said she couldn't make it. Something about one of her ex-husbands stopping by unexpectedly."

Now Erin joined the group. "One of her ex-husbands? Leigh, how many times has the woman been married?"

Leigh sighed. Sheesh. "I don't know. Two or three times, I guess."

"Which is it? Two or three?" Erin asked.

The back door to the kitchen opened, and Chase entered carrying a serving platter piled high with steaks. Behind him came Nathan...talking to Jared.

"This woman's been married six times," Chase said, shooting a nasty look at Leigh. "And I imagine you knew that when you set Jared up."

Oh, great. Now they were all going to gang up on her. Looking at Jared, she said, "You told me to find you women who were interested in marriage. Trisha is definitely interested in marriage."

Jared gave her a lopsided grin. "I said interested in marriage, not interested in making a career out of marriage. If I didn't know better, I'd start to think you didn't want to help me find my soulmate."

Like spectators at a tennis match, all her family's heads swiveled as they turned to look at her. Leigh groaned. "Hardly. You yourself have pointed out a couple of times that I'm bad at picking dates. Think about it. If I pick lousy ones for me, why wouldn't I also pick lousy ones for you?"

Without waiting for his answer, she grabbed the bowl of rolls and carried them into the dining room. She knew her response wouldn't slow her family down for long, but at least it would buy her a little time.

Personally, she was thrilled Jared hadn't even gone out with Trisha. She'd been a little worried about that. Ever since their kiss on Friday night, she'd decided she wasn't trying hard enough to get him to come around to her way of thinking.

Okay, so he wanted to settle down. But did it really have to be right away? And sure, he said he was done with his wild oats days, but maybe with the right enticement, he might consider spreading around just a few more of those oats.

At least it was worth a try. She'd failed last summer, but that didn't mean she couldn't give it another shot. Since she was stuck working with him anyway, she might as well enjoy herself.

It didn't take long before the rest of the group came out of the kitchen. Thankfully, they were carrying food and for a while only talked about dinner and work and nice, normal, non-aggravating subjects.

Until they all sat down.

"So are you going to keep letting Leigh set you up with women?" Megan asked as she passed the salad to Jared. "I think she has a solid point about her making poor choices."

Jared glanced at Leigh, a definite twinkle in his

brown eyes. "I don't know. I have to agree; she isn't very good at it."

Chase laughed. "Excuse me, but she fixed all of us up and did a fine job of it." He nailed Leigh with a direct look. "I think she's just not trying hard enough. I wonder why that is."

Leigh looked at Megan. "You have my sympathy. I didn't realize what a doof my brother was when I fixed you up with him."

Megan laughed. "That's okay. I like doofs."

Deciding the best offense was a good defense, Leigh said, "It's not my turn to fix up Jared. It's his turn to fix me up with one of his friends. Let's see if he's any better at this than I am."

Truthfully, she didn't want to go out with one of Jared's friends. Deep down, she was hoping he'd get jealous and call the whole thing off.

Instead, he nodded. "That's true. So, Leigh, what are you doing Tuesday night?"

That took her by surprise. Apparently, he'd already given this some thought. Darn him. "Why so soon? There's no rush."

"We have the parade meeting tomorrow night, and then we need to start building the floats this weekend. Homecoming is the end of next week. We don't have a lot of time," Jared said. "Besides, he's really anxious to go out with you, so Tuesday seems like the best choice."

Erin was sitting on Leigh's left, and she handed her the tossed salad. "So, are you busy? Are you going to go out with this guy?"

"I'm thinking," Leigh said.

Wow, Tuesday was so soon. She didn't have time to really think this over, to dangle it in front of Jared and try to make him jealous.

But since her entire blasted family was looking at her, waiting for an answer, she sighed. "Fine. I'll go out with this guy. But tell him I can't stay out late because Wednesday is a school day."

"Duly noted," Jared said. Then he smiled. One of those I-know-something-you-don't-know smiles.

Leigh started to tell him this better not be a joke when she noticed that Megan was almost as green as the lettuce in the salad. "Hey, Megan, are you okay? You look odd."

Megan didn't say a word. Instead, she jumped from her chair and sprinted out of the room. Chase was right behind her, leaving the rest of them staring at each other.

Stunned, Leigh spun around to stare at Nathan and Trent. "She's pregnant?"

"I don't know." Nathan looked at Emma. "Is she?"

Emma shrugged. "Beats me." She looked at Erin. "Have you heard anything?"

Erin shook her head. "Nope." She looked at Trent. "You?"

"Not a word," Trent said.

Something in the way Jared was sitting so silently made Leigh look at him. Unlike the rest of them, he didn't seem a bit surprised. "You know something, don't you?"

Jared merely said, "You should ask Chase and Megan."

Leigh gaped at him. "You do know something. How come out of everyone in this room, you're the first to know that Megan is pregnant?"

"I didn't say she's pregnant," Jared countered. "You said that."

"But you didn't say she isn't pregnant." Leigh leaned back in her chair. Chase sure had come to like Jared if he'd already told the other man about Megan's pregnancy—even before he'd told his own family.

Chase came back into the room then, and everyone asked almost in unison, "Is Megan pregnant?"

Chase got a dopey grin on his face. "Yep."

Emma and Erin went after Megan, leaving Leigh alone with her brothers and Jared.

"Wow, a baby," she said as she walked over and hugged Chase. "Congrats."

Chase hugged her back. "Thanks."

Leigh found her gaze drifting to Jared and found him looking straight at her.

For a split second, she could read it all in his eyes. His desire to be in Chase's place, happily married with a baby on the way.

Understanding hit Leigh like a right hook. Jared was trying to get her to change her mind about falling in love and getting married. She was going to all this trouble to get him to change his mind, while at the same time, he was trying to change hers.

And since he was trying to change her mind about dating and having fun, that meant that whoever her blind date was with Tuesday night was probably going to be missing his front teeth and apt to scratch himself while they were being served the entree.

Leigh bit back a laugh. They were playing a game. Winner takes all.

What Jared hadn't counted on was that she was very, very good at games. And she wasn't about to lose this one.

On Monday night, Jared had barely entered the gym

when Mary Monroe cornered him. "Do you know how to make a giant X on me?"

Okay, he'd come to expect a lot of weird things from this town, but he hadn't expected Mary's question.

"Maybe your husband should do that instead," he said when she kept staring at him, obviously expecting an answer.

"No, he can't. Ted's going to ask Leigh to make a giant R on him, and I need someone to make a giant X on me, or it won't be fair."

Dang. At times like this, he couldn't help thinking his brain had been addled a little too much while on the rodeo circuit.

He raised his hands. "Mary, I give up. I haven't a clue what you're asking me to do or even why you'd want me to do it."

Mary give him a look that made it clear she thought he was denser than a log. "Ted and I are going to walk in the parade, and since we own the drugstore, we thought it would be cute if he had an R on him, and I had an X on me. We thought we'd wear black leotards and have the letters written on us in chalk."

Oh, now it made some sort of twisted sense. "I see," he said, although the thought of Ted and Mary

Monroe walking around in leotards was enough to make him shudder.

"I have a thought. Rather than having the letters drawn on you, why don't you wear sandwich boards? That way, you'll have signs both on your front and your back, so people watching the parade can clearly see you. And you won't need anyone to draw letters on you. You can make the signs yourself."

Not to mention, the whole town would be spared the view of the couple barely dressed.

"I don't know." She turned to look at the man who'd wandered over to join them, Earl Guthrie, mayor of Honey. "What do you think, Earl? Should Ted and I wear a sandwich board?"

Earl took off his glasses and slowly cleaned them on his shirt. He appeared to be giving Mary's question serious consideration, but Jared had a feeling the older man was just stalling for time.

Finally, Earl put his glasses back on and then looked at Mary. "I think a sandwich board would be the best approach. It certainly would be easier for people in the crowd to see. The chalk could rub off you."

Apparently, since Earl was the one now offering the opinion, Mary decided to accept it.

"Yes, I see what you mean. I don't want everyone confused as to what Ted and I are doing," she said.

"Well, let me go tell Ted, so he doesn't waste his time asking Leigh to write on him."

As she walked away, Earl said, "I think the entire town owes us a hardy thanks, don't you?"

Jared nodded. "Absolutely."

He watched Mary make her way to the other side of the room, and then his gaze landed on Leigh. She looked so pretty tonight with her dark hair pulled back from her face with clips. She was laughing at something someone had said, and Jared couldn't help smiling.

Damn, she was beautiful. And that kiss she'd given him had rocked him clear to his soul. Now, more than ever, he was determined to work things out between them.

"I guess I'm standing here talking to myself," Earl noted. "I don't think you've heard a word I've said. You're too busy making cow eyes at Leigh."

"Hey, I'm not making cow eyes," Jared said. "I was just..." He floundered for an excuse. Finally, he sighed. "Sorry, Earl, didn't mean to ignore you."

Earl grinned. "That's quite all right. I was young once upon a time. I know how difficult it is for a man to concentrate when a certain woman is around. Why, one time, I was so besotted that I forgot where I parked my car. No matter how hard I tried, I couldn't remember where I'd left the thing."

"What happened?"

"I married her." Earl chuckled at the odd look Jared gave him. "I mean the woman, not the car. I eventually found my car three blocks from my house. Why I left it there, I'll never know. Must have been too busy thinking about love."

"Hey, don't you go around town telling stories to everyone that I'm in love and especially not who I was looking at," Jared said. "I'll get in trouble."

"Secrets stay secrets with me," Earl said.

Jared believed that. He'd always liked and admired Earl, and the rest of the town must have, too, because the man kept getting elected mayor.

"I'm having enough trouble getting the people in this town to forgive my past indiscretions," Jared explained. "I keep getting them pointed out to me everywhere I go. Guess I underestimated how long memories last."

Earl scratched his bald head and looked thoughtful. "Well, some folks must be warming up to you a mite. Take Mary Monroe. She just asked you to draw a big X on her body. Seems pretty warmed up to me."

Jared laughed. The older man had a point. "Maybe she thought I'd be the only one willing to do something so outrageous."

"Could be. But don't let the gossip get you down. Hang in there. Sooner or later, I'm sure these folks will thaw and stop bringing up every little thing you ever did wrong. You're one of us. You were born here in Honey. Raised here. And you showed a lot of gumption moving back." He fixed Jared with a steady look. "I admire gumption."

Jared really appreciated the older man's support. "Thanks, Earl."

Earl patted him on the shoulder. "You bet. I'm glad you came home." Then, with a conspiratorial smile and a quick glance at Leigh, he added, "And good luck with all your endeavors. I have a feeling you've chosen a tough goal with that one, but it will be worth it. You'll see. My Fran took some convincing, but we've been together almost fifty years."

With that, Earl wandered off. Jared looked over at Leigh. Yep, he'd chosen a tough goal with her. But as Earl said, it would be worth it, no matter what it took.

That kiss had convinced him he couldn't give up.

7

Leigh opened her front door and wasn't a bit surprised to see Jared standing on the doorstep.

"I don't believe this. You're my date?" Although she tried to sound disappointed and upset, it wasn't easy. She'd been hoping Jared would come himself instead of sending one of his friends. The more time she spent with Jared, the more she wanted him. So much so that she'd given up the idea of enjoying her freedom with other guys.

For the moment, the only guy she wanted to be with was Jared.

He leaned against the doorjamb, looking too sexy for words in his jeans and T-shirt. A slow, lazy grin crossed his face. "I ran into a little trouble thinking of guys who'd be willing to go out with you."

"Hey!" She shoved his arm. "A lot of men find me very attractive."

Men like him. She could tell from the appreciative way his gaze skimmed her little black dress that he was enjoying the view very much. Yahoo! Looked like seducing Jared wasn't going to be too difficult after all.

"Oh, you won't get any argument from me. You're good-looking, but at times you can be..."

When he didn't continue, she prompted, "Witty? Enticing? Intriguing?"

He chuckled. "Stubborn. So I couldn't fix you up with just anyone. He had to be tough."

Leigh rolled her eyes. "Give me a break. You didn't even try to find me a date, did you?"

"No. I did. But the problem was, how to find you a date that was as...unique as the ones you found for me. Most of the guys I know are fairly normal. Although Barry Olsen can make the exotic dancer tattoo on his belly shimmy like a real woman. I considered setting you up with him, but he's up in Wyoming at the moment. Sorry."

Pretending to be disappointed, she said, "Some friend you are. Well, I guess I'll see you at the parade meeting tomorrow night. Remember, everyone's coming to your place to start assembling the floats. And whatever you do, keep an eye on Tommy and

Kate. Those two disappeared twice last night. Who knows what they were up to."

Jared winked. "I have a fairly good idea what they were up to."

"Yeah, well, they need to cut it out, so help me keep tabs on them, okay?"

He nodded. "Fine. But what about tonight? You're not seriously going to stay home. Not when I'm standing here, more than willing to be your date."

Leigh put her hands on her hips and slowly studied his clothes. Although he looked gorgeous in his jeans and T-shirt, he was hardly dressed to match her.

"Gee, as tempting as it sounds to go to the local hamburger joint and have a milkshake, I think I'll pass."

"Whoa. Whoa." Jared stopped the door from closing. "Come on. Change out of that slinky dress and into jeans, and I'll take you for a ride on my Harley."

That made her stop. Slowly, she turned back to face him. Now this could definitely work in her favor.

"Will you teach me how to drive it?" she asked.

Jared laughed. "You're kidding, right?"

Leigh reached out and tugged the door free from his grip. "Say good night, Kendrick."

Once again, Jared stopped her from shutting the

door. "Fine. Fine. If you're serious about learning to drive one, I'll run you through the basics tonight, then we'll go to dinner. If you still want to learn after that, I'll teach you once we're done with the homecoming parade. Deal?"

Leigh grinned. This was perfect. Absolutely perfect. "Good. And just so you know, I'm holding you to that promise. Learning to ride a motorcycle is one of the three things I most want to do now that I have my freedom."

He gave her a devilish smile. "Of course, I now have to ask what the other two things are."

Leigh didn't plan on telling all her secrets at once. She had him intrigued. She planned on keeping him that way.

As far as she was concerned, this game they were playing had just started. He might think he could change her mind about settling down, but he was wrong. But that didn't mean she couldn't change his mind about having an affair.

She was very good at getting what she wanted. "Give me a moment, and I'll go change my clothes." Without waiting for his answer, she sprinted toward her bedroom. She knew exactly what to wear that would get Jared's motor racing. Tugging on her favorite snug jeans, she added the new red sweater she'd bought last week. The sweater was a little too short to reach the top of her jeans, so a small strip of her stomach showed between the two.

That ought to get him.

Wandering out a few minutes later, she found Jared prowling her living room like a bored lion. He turned when she entered, then froze.

His gaze was heated as he studied her outfit. "Man, you look..." He blinked. Twice. "Good. You look good."

The way he said the word good made it clear he meant she looked hot. "Thanks."

Biting back a smile, she walked over and tugged her keys out of her purse. Stuffing the key to her house in the front pocket of her jeans, she then turned to face him.

"So where are we having dinner?"

Jared's attention was riveted to the small strip of skin showing between her jeans and her top.

"I can't help wondering if your belly button is pierced," he murmured.

Since the top of her jeans just covered her navel, she knew he couldn't see. At first, she started to tell him no, but then a better idea occurred to her.

"I guess you'll have to find out for yourself," she teased, liking the way he looked at her with such heat and intent in his gaze.

A slow seductive smile crossed his face. "Is that a challenge?"

She tipped her head and pretended to consider his question. "Take it any way you want."

Jared chuckled. "Tonight should be interesting."

She couldn't agree more. Wanting to get started, she reached over and grabbed his hand. "Come on. I want you to teach me how to drive a motorcycle before it gets dark."

Jared wrapped his hand around hers, and then to her surprise, tugged her close. Leigh's breath caught in her throat, and she tipped her head to look up at him.

"Just a second, okay?" His voice was soft and smooth and deep, and Leigh's heart pounded in her chest. Ever so slowly, he leaned down until his lips were a whisper away from hers.

"I wonder if anything else on you is pierced," he said softly.

Then he kissed her, his tongue gliding inside her mouth. With an eek, Leigh wrapped her arms around his neck and kissed him back. Wow. This man could kiss. She couldn't remember ever being kissed so thoroughly.

In fact, she was so busy kissing Jared that it took a minute for her to realize that the hand he had at her waist had dipped beneath the waistband of her jeans and was now exploring her navel. At his touch, the air seemed to catch in Leigh's throat.

As his wandering hand continued to explore, she did the only thing a self-respecting modern female could do. She slipped the fingers of one of her hands under the waistband of his jeans.

Jared broke the kiss and with a chuckle, said, "Guess we both now know the other doesn't have a pierced navel."

She flashed him a grin. "Or a pierced tongue."

For the tenth or eleventh time, Jared shook his head. "No, Leigh, that's the brake. You just don't seem to be paying attention."

Man, that was an understatement. No matter how many times he ran her through the parts of the motorcycle, she didn't seem to remember them. Normally, he'd think it was because she really wasn't interested in learning. But tonight, he figured she was as distracted as he was. That kiss had been wild. And they both knew good and well that a kiss like that promised more to come later.

He could hardly wait.

Walking up behind her, he wrapped his arms around her waist. "Tell me another one of those things you've always wanted to do," he whispered in her ear. "Maybe we'll have better luck with it."

She leaned back against him. "Before I do, I want you to know I won't marry you."

He'd expected her to mention this sooner or later. He knew very well how she currently felt about love and marriage. That didn't mean he wasn't sure she'd eventually change her mind.

"Did I ask you to marry me? Seems to me we were talking about something else," he pointed out.

Leigh turned within the circle of his arms until she faced him. "Okay. So we're clear on this. If we're going to do any more of what we were doing earlier, I want it clearly understood that we're just messing around."

Jared leaned down until his forehead rested against hers. "Yes. I agree. We're just messing around. Now tell me another thing on your list."

He must have sounded pretty convincing because she said, "I want to go to one of those wild, crazy nightclubs in Dallas and dance."

That was something he could easily do. "Fine. Let's go then."

With a squeal, Leigh threw her arms around his neck and kissed him hard. "I like a man who is so agreeable."

Jared got on his motorcycle, and then helped her on as well. Yep, he planned on being agreeable. Very, very agreeable. So agreeable that pretty soon, Leigh would fall in love with him—whether she wanted to or not.

Then they'd talk about that whole getting married thing again.

He handed her one of the helmets, then put on his. "Wear that. You may want to use your brains later on in life."

She laughed but did as he said. "Harhar."

"Now hold on to me," he told her. As soon as she wrapped her arms around his waist, he started the engine. Leigh immediately scooted closer to him and held him tighter. He loved the feeling of her pressed against him. So soft and warm.

"Drive really fast," she said into his left ear.

Jared chuckled. Leave it to Leigh to want to be fast and wild. He headed out of town and more or less did what she asked. It would take them over an hour to get to Dallas if they didn't get stopped for speeding. And he didn't want to get stopped. Not tonight. He had too many things planned.

So he kept Leigh moving. Through dinner at a cozy little Italian restaurant, then club hopping. When they ended up at a completely insane place, he kept her close. Speaking of piercings, he and Leigh seemed to be the only people who didn't have their lips and noses pierced.

"This place makes me feel a hundred years old," Jared yelled to Leigh.

Leigh was standing in the middle of the dance floor, staring at people as they went by. "I know what you mean."

When a man danced by with hair spiked so high it looked like spears, she shuddered. "Let's go home."

About time. Jared snagged her hand and pulled her through the crowd. He'd been waiting to head home for the past two hours.

When they reached his Harley, he once again handed her a helmet. She flashed him a sexy grin.

"Thanks for making two of my three wishes come true," she told him. Then she leaned against him and kissed his chin. "I'm really enjoying this date. It's so much more fun when you're part of the date rather than merely ruining it."

He chuckled. "Gee, thanks. I'll keep that in mind."

"Have I told you tonight that I think you're a really nice guy?"

Her compliment caught him by surprise. He honestly couldn't remember anyone ever calling him nice and sincerely meaning it. "I don't think many people will agree with you on that one."

"They will. Eventually."

Unable to resist, he leaned down and kissed her. He wrapped his arms around her and poured all the love and desire he felt for this woman into his kiss. It must have been pretty good because several people in the parking lot started hooting and hollering at them, cheering him on.

He broke the kiss when a kid with purple and pink hair slapped him on the back and told him to "Go for it, dude."

"Um, thanks," Jared told the enthusiastic spectator.

Leigh was laughing as they got on the motorcycle. "This place is insane."

"Many days Honey doesn't seem much better." She leaned against him, wrapping her arms around his waist. "So are you going to do what he suggested?"

Jared wanted to think he knew what she was talking about, but he'd learned long ago to never make assumptions when it came to Leigh.

"What would that be?"

"Go for it, dude. I think it sounds like a wonderful idea."

Jared grinned. "Sounds like a plan to me."

The second Jared turn off the Harley and helped her down, she wrapped herself around him. No sense giving him the chance to change his mind.

Although from the way he was kissing her back, he wasn't changing his mind anytime soon.

"Where's the key?" he asked between kisses. "I don't want the entire town of Honey watching us."

"It's almost midnight. Most of Honey is asleep," she teased, reaching into her pocket to get the key. It wasn't there, so she tried the other front pocket.

"Uh-oh."

Jared had been kissing her neck, but now he leaned back to look at her in the light from her front porch. "Uh-oh, what?"

"Uh-oh, I seem to have lost the key. Must have been when I was dancing at one of those places in Dallas. Well, we won't worry about it. My address isn't on it, so no one will ever know what door it fits. Let's go back to kissing some more."

Jared blew out a deep breath and gently held her away. "Seriously, we can't stand in front of your house doing this. Since you're trying to land a teaching job, I doubt if necking with the town's bad boy will help."

He had to be kidding. "You're not changing your mind, are you? Please tell me you're not changing your mind."

"No. But before we go any further, let's head to my house."

She put her hands on her hips. "That's too far away. Let's just break in."

"I'm not breaking into your house," he said. "Who else has a key?"

She held up one hand and ticked off their options. "My big brother Chase. My other big brother Nathan. And my last big brother Trent, who also happens to be the chief of police. Which one do you think we should call?"

"None of them," Jared muttered. "One look at the two of us, and whichever of your brothers stops by will string me up from the nearest tree."

"You're probably right. At the least, they'd insist you head on home before they unlock my house." She glanced around. Of all the stupid times to lose her key. She wanted inside this house now.

She knew if she didn't think fast, Jared would change his mind. He'd say it was for the best, and then he'd kiss her and get all noble, call one of her brothers and leave once she was inside her house. All alone. And frustrated.

Not on his life. Even though he was pretending he didn't care that all they were having was a fling, she knew he felt differently. She could feel what he felt in his touch, see it in his gaze.

And sure, she cared for him, too. Not in the "till-death-do-us-part way," but deeply. He probably wouldn't believe her if she told him this, but she wouldn't want to make love with him if she didn't care about him.

But caring and marrying were two verrrrry different concepts.

Jared was looking at his watch. "Leigh, it's late. Maybe we should do this some other time. Why don't we call one of your brothers? I'll stick around until they show up and let you in."

Leigh snorted. "As if. You said you'd make love with me, and I'm not letting you off the hook, buddy."

Jared chuckled. "Takes a particular kind of woman to say something like that to a man."

Leigh nudged past him. "Yeah, well, I expect you to honor your promise." She tugged on the doorknob. "Stupid door. Stupid key."

When she glanced back at him, he was studying her. "When exactly did I promise to make love with you?"

He seriously couldn't have changed his mind, could he? She looked him up and down. From what she could see, he still was very interested in the whole making love idea.

"Hey, you agreed to go for it, dude. If that isn't a

promise, I don't know what is." She tugged on the doorknob again. "Besides I bought a brand-new red lace bra today that I'm currently wearing, and I'd like your opinion on it."

Jared made a groaning noise and took a step toward her. Leigh laughed and held up one hand. "Down, boy."

Then she quickly amended, "Forget I said that. But give me a second here. The locks on my house aren't very good. I know you know how to break in."

He frowned. "What do you mean the locks aren't very good? Leigh, even though you live in a small town, you have to be careful. First thing tomorrow, I'm changing your locks. You're going to be safe."

She bobbed her head. "Good idea. You do that. Right after you break in tonight and check out my red bra."

Jared glanced around. "I don't know."

Oh, for pity's sake. "Hello," she said, then once he was looking at her, pulled aside the neckline of her sweater and flashed him a little peek at her bra. "Passionate lovemaking awaits inside."

Jared made another groaning sound, then immediately set about examining the lock. Eureka. Nothing like flashing a man your undies to get him in gear.

"Which door is easier, the front or the back?" he

asked, and she didn't miss that his voice was raspy with desire.

"I guess they're both the same. I've never rated them on an easy-to-jimmy scale, so it's hard to say."

"Very funny." He examined the front door. "Opening this will be a piece of cake. You keep an eye out."

"You bet." Then just to make certain he didn't lose his motivation, she proceeded to whisper naughty suggestions in his ear the entire time he was fiddling with the lock.

"We're going to get caught," he told her, but not with any conviction in his voice.

"I'm breaking into my own house, and everyone around here knows it's my house. What's the worst they can do to me?" She leaned forward and nibbled on his earlobe. "Put me under house arrest? I'd welcome it at this moment."

Before Leigh could torment him much more, he threw open her front door and tugged her inside.

"That is the worst excuse for a lock I've ever seen," he told her as he pushed the door closed and relocked it.

Leigh turned on the lamp by the couch, then pulled her red sweater over her head. She stood before him in a skimpy red lace bra and low-riding jeans. "Was it worth it?"

Jared grinned. "In the morning, remind me to write that company and thank them for making such a crummy lock."

She grinned back. Tonight was going to be serious fun.

✹ 8 ✺

"**Y**ou have a hickey," Emma said.

Leigh, Erin, and Emma were helping with last-minute touches on some of the floats. The parade was rapidly approaching, and at the moment, Leigh was painting what she hoped looked like a panther on the side of the float Nathan's business was entering.

Leaning back, she surveyed her handiwork. Yep. It looked like one big, black ferocious...inkblot.

"I have an idea. Let's make Nathan's float a giant Dalmatian. Then my black blobs will make sense," Leigh suggested.

Emma tapped her on the shoulder. "You're ignoring my comment. Young lady, you have a hickey on your neck. Where in the world would you get something like that?"

"Hickeys Are Us," she said, leaning back and surveying the panthers Erin was painting. They looked like panthers. "I nominate Erin to do all the panther painting from now on. Who seconds my nomination?"

She glanced expectantly at Emma, who merely gave her a pointed look. This was the problem with being friends with the wives of your brothers. If you told them something, then you were also telling your brothers. And she for one did not want her brothers knowing she'd spent the last evening having unbelievable fun with Jared.

"Emma, if you don't get back to work, I'm going to tell Nathan that you're goofing off and that I need more volunteers from his company to help," Leigh said.

Emma laughed. "Oh, right. Tell him that. And I'll tell him that you have a big hickey on the side of your neck and a goofy smile on your face. He's a bright man. He'll quickly figure out what's going on."

Leigh snorted. "Pulleese. It took him forever to figure out he was in love with you."

Erin walked over and poured more black paint in her tray. As she was about to walk away, she said, "Hey, Leigh, you have a big red mark on your neck."

"It's a birthmark," Leigh muttered.

"It's a hickey," Emma corrected.

Erin tipped her head and studied it. "You know, I don't think so. I think it's beard burn." She looked at Emma. "I think someone who has a beard was kissing Leigh's neck recently."

Emma leaned over and inspected the mark. "I think you're right. And it seems to disappear beneath the collar of her shirt, which leads me to believe it's on more than just her neck. Now who does Leigh know who would have a beard and would want to kiss her?"

Erin tipped her head. "That's a good question, but I have no idea. The last I heard, she wasn't seeing anyone." She examined Leigh's neck again. "But she sure is now. And he certainly is attracted to our Leigh."

"Cute. Very cute." Standing, Leigh brushed off her jeans. "Since I'm no use at painting the panthers, and I have no intention of telling either of you anything, I think I'll go see if I can help Steve Myerson get his wagon ready to pull Rufus in."

She was all set to walk away when Emma said, "Looks like it won't be long before there's another wedding."

That stopped her cold. She walked over to where her sisters-in-law were working and said firmly, "No. Don't even think that. Don't even think about thinking that. In fact, forget you ever knew how to think. There will be no wedding. Got it? I'm just having a little fun. Heck, I haven't even graduated from college yet. I'm not getting married."

Emma looked at Erin, who shrugged. "All I was going to say was that the church books up early. You need to plan these things a long time in advance."

Grrr. "Read my lips—there isn't going to be a wedding."

Once again, she started to walk away when Erin said, "You know, I didn't want to fall in love. I mean, I really, really didn't. How about you, Emma?"

Emma nodded. "Me, neither. I didn't have time to fall in love. I had my life all mapped out. And I was happy. Or at least, I thought I was happy. But then someone convinced me I was being an idiot." She pretended to think. "Now who was that?"

Erin smiled. "I know, it's baffling, isn't it? Who was the person who made certain we all admitted it when we'd fallen in love?"

Oh, for pity's sake. "I'm not in love. He's not in love. We're not in love. It's sex. Pure and simple. Now paint some panthers."

Emma studied Leigh, then finally said, "Okay. If you say this is just about sex, then we'll leave you alone. But remember, life doesn't always work out the way you have planned. You have to be flexible if you don't want happiness to pass you by."

Erin nodded. "I couldn't agree more."

Leigh liked these ladies; she really did. But boy, they were wrong about her. She was having the time of her life, enjoying her freedom, savoring her independence. She wasn't giving that up for anyone. Not even for Jared Kendrick.

Deciding the best way to avoid talking about love anymore was to, well, avoid it, Leigh headed across the room. Billy had finished his cow car, so she figured she'd go check it out. It wasn't every day you got to see a 1997 sedan decked out like a cow. Udders and all.

Truthfully, it had turned out kinda cute. Well, for a cow car. She was all set to walk away when a muted giggle caught her attention. Stopping, she strained to hear over the noise in the barn. Maybe she'd been mistaken.

She took another two steps and heard it again. Someone was giggling. And they were doing it inside the cow.

Oh, for the love of Pete. She needed this aggravation like she needed to go cross-eyed.

Although she didn't want the entire barn to know what was happening, Leigh wanted those two lovestruck teenagers out of that car right now. She rapped on the side of the cow. "Get out here."

A couple of "shushes" was all she got in return.

Leigh rapped again. "Tommy and Kate, I know you're in there. Get out now."

She still got no reaction and was about to knock again when Jared wandered over. "You mad at the cow? Maybe I can help improve your mood."

Although she was happy to see him, now was not the time to flirt with Jared. She wanted those kids out of that car right this instant.

"Tommy and Kate are in there." She blew out a breath of disgust. The only saving grace to this mess was that most of the crowd had already left for the evening.

But still, she wasn't in the mood to do this. She glanced at Jared. She was in the mood to do...well, him.

As much as she'd like to, she couldn't think about that right now. She had to do something about Tommy and Kate.

"You can't stay in that cow forever," she pointed out.

With a lot of moaning and groaning, first Tommy, then Kate crawled out from under the tarps covering Billy Joe's car. Predictably, the kids looked a mess.

Tommy smoothed his hair away from his face. "Hi, Ms. Barrett. The float looks cool, doesn't it?"

"The only thing that needs to cool around here is you and Kate," Leigh said. "This is crazy. You two need to cut it out." She looked at Kate. "Have you told your father you're seeing Tommy?"

Kate shook her head. "I think he'd have a stroke."

Yes, that was a possibility. "You still have to tell your parents." She looked at Tommy. "You, too."

Tommy groaned and scuffed one sneaker on the ground. "Why? Kate and I are in love. If we tell people, they'll just get all huffy and tell us we're too young to be in love. Then they'll do everything they can to get us to stop seeing each other."

He moved over and draped one arm around Kate's shoulders. "We're old enough to recognize true love when we find it. Not a lot of people can say that, but we can."

Leigh was trying to formulate a response when Jared jumped in.

"If you're truly in love, you shouldn't be hiding in a cow," Jared told him. "Be proud of what you feel and tell the people in your life. Tommy, your folks love you. So do yours, Kate. I'm sure if you two agree to handle your relationship responsibly, your parents will let you date." He gave Tommy a pointed look. "And responsibly doesn't mean hiding in closets or home-coming floats."

Both Tommy and Kate nodded. "Okay, I'll tell my parents," Kate said. "Dad will have a fit, but he'll probably calm down. Eventually."

Leigh looked at Tommy. "What about you?"

"Yeah, I'll tell them, mostly because then Kate and I can let everyone know we're in love."

In a way, the two of them were really sweet. Of course, Leigh didn't believe for a second what they felt was true love. But they believed it, and she knew no one would be able to change their minds.

"Okay, now that we've settled this, I think both of you need to head home and tell your parents tonight. Frankly, I'm tired of hunting you down," Leigh said.

Kate sighed. "Okay. I'll tell Dad. Maybe he won't get so upset if I tell him that one day, Tommy and I are going to get married."

With that, the two teens headed for the door. "You think Gavin is going to be happy to hear his daughter's planning on marrying Tommy Tate someday?" Jared asked dryly.

"No. Especially when he figures out that then she'll be Kate Tate."

Jared chuckled. "True. But you can't stop love."

Grrr. Leigh was tired of talking about love. Really tired of it. She glanced around Jared's barn. Her sisters-in-law had obviously been watching the entire confrontation with Tommy and Kate. Oh great. Now they'd quote Jared's comments about love to her.

"I think it's time we sent everyone home," she told him.

Jared nudged her. "Are you going to keep me after, teacher?"

She shouldn't. Considering all the talk about love floating around this barn, she should head on home. But then Jared gave her a slow, sexy grin, and her common sense got vapor-locked by the desire fogging up her brain. Her gaze dropped to his oh-so delicious mouth.

Yep, there were lots of reasons she should go home alone tonight, but thankfully, not a single one came to mind.

So, after Emma and Erin finally left, laughing and singing "Love is a Many Splendored Thing" off-key, Leigh turned to Jared and said, "Just so you know, I'm not going to fall in love with you."

Jared's expression didn't change a bit. "The thought never crossed my mind."

Oh right, like she believed that. But no matter what he thought, she really wasn't going to fall in love with him.

No matter what he, her family, and the population of Honey thought.

It just wasn't going to happen.

"Your plan isn't working."

Jared had been brushing his favorite horse, Spirit, but now he turned and looked at Trent Barrett. The parade was going to start any second. Leigh's brother should be helping with crowd control.

He glanced at the few folks on the sidewalk and the tons of people lined up in the parade. Okay, so the spectators weren't exactly going to be a problem. But someone had to keep this parade in line, so Mary and Ted Monroe walked next to each other and didn't wander off to talk to friends, leaving everyone wondering what the letters on them meant.

And someone needed to tell the band teacher that she could play the "Hokey Pokey" all she wanted, but his horses weren't going to shake it all about.

"What exactly are you talking about?" he asked Trent. "And why aren't you helping Leigh line people up? I'm the end of the parade." He patted Spirit's rump. "Remember?"

"I'll get up there in a second. First, I want to talk to you. Erin told me what you said to Tommy and Kate in the barn. You need to take your own advice. Carpe diem, Jared. Seize the day."

He'd like to seize the day, but if he did, Leigh would more than likely seize his neck—and squeeze. "Things aren't that simple."

"If you love her, tell her so," Trent said. "That's pretty simple."

"It's not simple at all." Jared brushed Spirit a couple more times. He'd like to tell her, but she kept making it crystal clear that she didn't want to discuss love. Even when they were making mind-blowing love, she didn't want the words.

Getting her to admit she loved him was going to take some doing.

Trent sighed. "You know, I went through the same sort of thing with Erin. I fell for her a long time before she fell for me. It was tough. But I hung in there. I let her know how I felt, and I stood my ground. You need to tell Leigh you love her and that you're going to keep loving her whether she likes it or not."

Jared chuckled. "That ought to show her."

Reaching into his shirt pocket, Trent pulled out a pair of sunglasses. He slipped them on, then said to Jared, "No one ever said love was easy. But it is worth all the trouble. Man, is it ever."

With that, he headed toward the front of the parade. Jared could hear him shouting at the panthers from Bud's Boats and Baits to keep their paws off the panthers from Patty's Powder and Primp.

But at the moment, his mind wasn't on the parade. It was on what Trent had said. Should he stand his ground and confront Leigh about his feelings? Would it do any good, or would it make Custer's last stand look successful?

He turned and told the other two riders, Stan and Dwayne, to saddle up. He'd have to think about what to do with Leigh later. Right now, he had a parade to ride in.

Even if his horses still couldn't do the "Hokey Pokey."

⚜

"Before we begin tonight's halftime show, I'd like to take a minute to recognize some of our volunteers," Gavin said into the microphone.

Leigh rocked her weight from heel to heel as Gavin's speech droned on. She didn't know why she had to be here. She'd already done her part. She'd coordinated the parade yesterday, which if she did say so herself, had turned out great. No one got hurt. Everyone had fun.

What else could you ask from a successful parade?

Tonight was the homecoming game, followed by the student dance. Then tomorrow night, the alumni got their chance to pretend they still were young at their own dance.

But her part was done. And she wanted to go home and be with Jared.

She glanced at the man in question. He looked as anxious to leave as she was. Good. That meant they'd have another amazing night together.

She could hardly wait.

Unfortunately, Gavin had other ideas. He kept talking, and talking, and talking. Sigh. He first explained how important homecoming was to Honey High. Then he thanked everyone who'd helped make this weekend so exciting. Then he thanked the people of Honey for supporting the homecoming efforts.

And finally, he thanked the Honey Panthers themselves, who so far were ahead 21 to 3.

Wahoo. Go Panthers.

Finally, the speech ended, and Leigh and Jared headed off the platform.

"It didn't take me that long to finish high school," Jared murmured in her ear.

She laughed and was all set to see if he wanted to cut out and head back to her place when Gavin jogged over.

"Glad I caught you two. I want to talk about Kate."

Uh-oh. Leigh shifted until they were off the field and standing on a fairly deserted walkway. "Look, Gavin, I know you may not approve of Kate seeing Tommy—"

He blinked. "Why wouldn't I approve? The boy's got half the colleges in the country offering him scholarships. I'm sure he'll end up in the NFL."

Wow. That was the last thing Leigh had expected. She glanced at Jared, who seemed equally surprised.

"Glad to hear you feel that way," she said, bemused.

"Oh, don't get me wrong. I still want Kate to go to college and everything, but as long as she and Tommy don't do anything—" He shrugged. "You know. Then it's fine with me."

"Oh." Leigh smiled. "Good."

Gavin nodded. "Yes, it is. Kate's happy, so I'm happy. Love's a great thing."

Ah, crud, here they were with that love stuff again. All Leigh said in response was, "Hmmm."

Jared patted the other man on the shoulder. "Congratulations on homecoming weekend. It seems to be going well."

"It is. It is. Of course, naturally, the student dance sold out, but the alumni dance did, too. We really pulled them in this year. People are coming from all around."

"That's great," Leigh said, wishing he'd finish up so she and Jared could leave.

Gavin looked at her. "That's not all that's great. Leigh, I wanted to tell you that a full-time teaching position is waiting for you next year. You've really proven yourself with the parade."

Leigh hadn't been expecting him to offer her a job, well, certainly not so soon. She let out a yelp, then with a self-conscious laugh said, "Thanks. I really appreciate it."

"You earned it," he said. "Well, I've got to go see what my family is up to. And watch the game."

Gavin headed off, and Leigh commented, "Why do I get the feeling Kate will have a terrible time if she ever decides to break up with Tommy?"

"Yeah, it does seem like Gav's got his heart set on having a pro football player as a son-in-law." He nudged her. "Congratulations, teach. Looks like you got what you wanted."

Leigh grinned. "I did, didn't I? I got the job." She shot him a flirty glance. "And I got you. Yep, I'm one happy lady."

For a second, she simply enjoyed her feeling of pure bliss, then she noticed the odd look Jared was giving her.

"What?" she asked. "You got what you wanted, too. You have your rodeo school."

"Sort of. Right now I'm entertaining Steve's brother and his family. They're not really the kind of students I had in mind."

"But you're running your own business," she

pointed out. "And once you bring in enough money, you can afford to make your school the best around. Then you'll get lots and lots of rodeo students."

"True." Even though he'd agreed with her, he kept giving her that odd look.

"Oh, and let's not forget what else you have," she said, hoping to turn around his mood. "You've got me."

She leaned up, all set to give him a kiss, when he said, "No, I don't. I don't have you, Leigh."

Ah, jeez. She knew this was going to happen if everyone insisted on talking about love all the time. "Jared, we agreed—"

"No, you agreed. And I didn't argue. But here's the thing, Leigh. I love you. And I want to marry you."

She stared at him. This was much worse than she'd expected. Not only had he used the *L* word, but he'd gone and used the *M* word, too.

"Have you been thinking all along that I'll change my mind and suddenly decide I can't live without you?" she asked. "Was all this dating stuff some sort of plan, because if it was, it was a bad plan. And it didn't work."

Jared didn't seem upset with what she was saying. Just kinda resigned. "Fine. It may not have worked, but at least I gave it a shot."

Taking a step closer to her, he added, "You know, everyone in this town loves to point out to me all the things I've ever done wrong in my life. You'd think I was the only one in this town who ever made a mistake. But you know something? Loving you isn't a mistake, and nobody's going to tell me it is. Not even you. If you're too scared to give us a chance, then that's your mistake, not mine."

Leigh opened her mouth to say something, but he shook his head.

"Let me finish," he said. "I may not have all the answers, but I know one thing—you and I belong together. Not because I'm the bad boy in town, and I get your brothers upset. But because I love you more than any man ever will." He drew in a deep breath. "And what's really sad is deep down, you know I'm right. You're just too confused to admit it. Even to yourself."

With that, he turned and walked away from her. Leigh stared after him. Wow. She hadn't really expected that. Okay, that was a lie. She had sort of expected it. But she hadn't expected him to be so...sincere.

Well, he was wrong about her. About them. He might like to think that she loved him, but she didn't. She liked him. She liked him a lot. But that wasn't love.

Love was...a million clichés occurred to her, but that was all. Her mind was drawing a complete blank.

So she wasn't sure what love was, but she knew what it wasn't—it wasn't what she felt for Jared Kendrick.

Not at all.

9

"Don't you know how to tell time?" Leigh asked her brother Chase when she found him standing on her doorstep at seven the next morning. "It's Saturday. Some of us like to sleep in."

"Seven is sleeping in," he said. Then he shoved a pastry box at her. "Here. Stop being grumpy. I brought jelly doughnuts. That should keep you from biting my head off."

Leigh yawned—deliberately—and took the box. "Fine. You gave me the doughnuts. Thanks so much. Now can I go back to sleep?"

He chuckled. "To quote you, as if." Without first asking permission, he squeezed past her and headed toward the kitchen. "Got any coffee made?"

She so didn't need this today. The fight with Jared

had preyed on her mind, so she'd hardly gotten any sleep at all last night. All she wanted to do was curl up in bed and forget about everything.

"No, I don't have coffee made. Up until a couple of minutes ago, I was asleep." When Chase didn't answer, she padded after him. "Go home, Chase. I'm serious."

She found him making coffee. "Don't do that. You won't be here long enough to drink it. Take these doughnuts and go home. I'm sure Megan would like some breakfast, too."

"Megan's still asleep," he commented as he searched the cabinets. "Where do you keep your mugs?"

Grrr. She walked over and grabbed two mugs out of the cabinet next to the sink. "How come Megan gets to sleep in, and I don't?"

"Megan's pregnant. She needs her rest. You've got love life trouble, which you need to take care of." He started the coffee and sat at her small kitchen table. "So what are you going to do about Jared?"

She started to tell him it was none of his business, but then he said, "And how can I help?"

Oh, now what was a girl with a broken heart supposed to do when her big brother offered to help? Leigh sat down next to him.

"I guess somehow you know what happened last night at the stadium."

He nodded. "This is Honey. Everyone knows. A couple of folks overheard you."

Overheard. Spied on them. Same thing in Honey. With a groan, Leigh ran her hands through her hair. "Then they would have heard the part where I'm not interested in getting married. End of discussion. Jared and I want different things out of life. I thought we'd come to an agreement, but I guess not."

"I see," Chase said. "Go on."

"Go on? There's nothing more to go on to. We broke up. That's the end of the story." Although it bothered her admitting they were through, she'd just have to get used to it. Jared had known how she felt before they'd started dating. As far as she was concerned, it was dirty pool for him to try to change the rules now.

Chase stood and headed over to the coffeepot. Once he'd filled two mugs, he brought them to the table.

He shoved the mug with little hearts on it toward her. "Here."

Leigh shuddered. "It's black. I'd rather drink motor oil."

"Why drink coffee at all if you're going to gunk it

up with milk and sugar?" Chase took a big sip from his mug. "Yum."

"One man's yum is this woman's yuck," Leigh informed him. She headed over to the refrigerator and got out the milk. After pouring a healthy dose into her mug, she returned to her seat.

"So how is Megan doing? Still feeling sick?" she asked.

Chase chuckled. "Nice try, kiddo, but you're not changing the subject. Unlike you, Megan is fine."

"You know, I'm getting tired of you saying something is wrong with me. Just because I'm not interested in falling in love and getting married doesn't mean I'm the one who's wrong," she pointed out. Then, hoping if she were eating he'd leave her alone, she snagged a doughnut out of the box and took a big bite.

For a second, Chase just watched her. Then he said, "We boys never meant to make you miserable. Nathan, Trent, and I just wanted to take care of you 'cause you're our sister, and we love you. I'm sorry if we made you feel stifled."

This couldn't be Chase, the man who had single-handedly broken up most of her dates during high school, and even a couple during college.

She tapped the side of her head. "Excuse me? I must be hearing things. I thought you apologized."

Chase laughed. "Okay, okay. I know. It's not something I've done a lot in my life. Guess being married has mellowed me."

"Mellowed you. Not me. I'm still looking forward to having some fun and excitement in my life," she pointed out.

"You know, love and excitement are compatible, Leigh. You keep acting like if you fall in love, your life becomes dull and boring. That's just not true. Look at me. I'm about to become a dad. I don't think there's anything boring about that."

Leigh wanted to argue with him, but nothing came to mind. "I guess," she relented. "But it's not about that."

"It's about having your own way for once in your life, isn't it?" he asked. "Because you feel like Nathan, Trent, and I pushed you around, you now want to call the shots. That's understandable. And I won't lie to you, when you fall in love, you have to be willing to compromise. Not issue ultimatums like you did to Jared."

"Hey, I didn't issue an ultimatum," she maintained.

"The way I understand it, you told him not to fall in love with you, then got mad at him when he did. Sounds like an ultimatum to me."

Well, it wasn't. Not at all. It was...the rule for

their relationship. Okay, okay, her rule. Maybe she hadn't given him a lot of options. Or any options for that matter. Maybe she had said how she thought things should go and had expected that to be that.

She nibbled on her doughnut, suddenly unsure. Now that she thought about it, that didn't seem right. Or fair. Jared was a person, too. Why didn't he get some say in their relationship?

Grrr. More importantly, why did Chase have to point all this out to her and muddy waters she thought were crystal clear?

Chase stood. "Guess I'd better head on back home. You seem to be doing okay. I thought you'd be all weepy because you were never going to see Jared again. But you're just fine."

He leaned down and dropped a kiss on the top of her head. "See ya, kiddo. Don't forget, you're riding to the alumni dance with Megan and me."

Ah, jeez. The dance. She'd completely forgotten about the dance tonight.

"I don't think I'll go," she said.

Chase gave her a pointed look. "Now won't that give the town something to talk about? I can hear it now—Leigh Barrett had a big fight with Jared Kendrick, and now she's too ashamed to even show her face in public."

Leigh was beyond caring what everyone in Honey

thought. But sitting around her house wouldn't do her any good. And besides, she was starting to think she might owe Jared an apology. "Yeah, you're right. I've got no reason not to go."

She glanced at the clock. She'd need to get busy since she was going to the dance tonight. She wanted to be composed, and she didn't feel even remotely composed yet. She felt...sad. She might not be weepy like Chase had expected, but she was hurting. As much as she hated to admit it, she missed Jared. A lot.

And it had only been since yesterday.

She looked up at Chase. She was glad he'd stopped by, glad to know that her doofy brothers were always there for her. "Thanks."

"No thanks necessary. See you later, kiddo." Leigh nodded, but her mind was already on tonight. She could only hope that Jared intended on coming to the dance because she needed to talk to him.

She needed to talk to him badly.

❦

"But you have to come to the dance," Janet Defries said for about the millionth time.

Jared sighed. Why didn't the woman just take no for an answer and head on home? Her riding lesson had ended twenty minutes ago. It was time for her to leave.

But good manners kept him from kicking her out. Instead, he said patiently, "Janet, I'm not coming to the alumni dance. That's that."

"Because of Leigh Barrett? Oh, come on. You have to move on with your life. Get back on the horse."

"Pull myself up by my bootstraps?" he couldn't resist adding.

Janet frowned. "Don't tease. You have to come. The awards committee has something for you." She placed her hands on her hips and tried to look sexy. "Besides, you owe me a dance."

"Since when?" He started leading Spirit toward the barn, figuring Janet might finally get the hint.

Unfortunately, she didn't. She simply fell into step next to him. "Since the senior prom. I asked you to dance with me, and you said later. Well, it's later, Jared. You owe me a dance."

There was no way he was dancing with Janet. Or anyone else for that matter. All he wanted to do was stay home and take care of his ranch. He had no intention of going into Honey for a while.

He'd stay out here by himself. Well, by himself with Steve Myerson's brother and his family. And the family from Little Rock who'd heard about the new dude ranch and showed up on his doorstep today with no reservations but high hopes.

Dang. Even his business wasn't working out right. "I'm not going, Janet. Have a good time, though."

They'd reached the barn, and he started to head inside when she said, "So, that's it? Leigh says no, and you give up? The way I heard it, you told her you loved her and how things were going to be. But she threw your love back in your face. You can't hide out now. People will think you're a coward."

Jared considered what she said. He didn't really care what the people of Honey said. What bothered him was Janet's interpretation of what had happened. Had he really told Leigh how things were going to be?

Now that he thought about it, maybe he had. He hadn't said it would be okay for them to still be together even if she didn't want to get married. He hadn't said that he understood that she'd need time to think about what she wanted from their relationship.

He'd told her.

No wonder she'd told him no.

He missed her so much. He couldn't help thinking his plan had been dumb. He should have known better than to try to force her to fall in love with him.

He should have let her make her own decisions.

"I'll be at the dance," he said, his mind made up.

Behind him, Janet started talking about all the things they could do once he showed up at the dance, but he wasn't really listening.

All he could think about was seeing Leigh tonight.

"This isn't working," Jared said to Trent. He glanced at his watch. The dance had started twenty minutes ago, and she still wasn't there. It looked like Leigh was going to skip the dance just so she didn't have to see him.

"You worry too much. She'll come around. Just you wait," Trent said, getting a couple of glasses of punch.

"I agree. It's early," Erin said, taking one of the glasses of punch from her husband. "Wait and see what happens tonight."

Based on what had happened last night, he wasn't sure she'd even give him the chance to apologize. He figured one of two things would happen: either Leigh wouldn't show up or she'd show up, take one look at him, and walk the other way.

He hated both scenarios.

"Maybe I should head on home," he said.

Trent slapped him on the back. "Don't give up yet. The night's young. Lots of things can happen."

Jared watched as Trent and Erin set down their glasses and headed onto the dance floor. Yeah, lots of things could happen. Lots of bad things.

He glanced at his watch yet again. Maybe he could wait another fifteen minutes. But after that, he really was going to head home. He'd try to call her in a few days and see if she'd talk to him. Maybe if she cooled down, she'd give him a second chance.

Almost as if his mind were playing tricks on him, he heard her laughter floating down the hallway leading to the gym. She had come to the dance after all.

For a split second, he felt like he was seventeen again, waiting for the most popular girl in town to notice him. Except now, the stakes were much, much higher. He wanted the woman he loved to forgive him.

And he figured he had about as much chance of that happening as he did of flying by flapping his arms. Still, he tensely waited for Leigh to appear in the doorway.

When she did enter, she looked amazing. She had on a long black dress that shimmered when she walked. The dress hugged her figure, draping over her curves and skimming down her long legs.

Desire hit him hard, followed by longing. Dang, he missed her.

After staring at Leigh for a long, long time, he finally noticed that Chase and Megan were with her. Focusing on Leigh, he waited for her to spot him. When she did, he expected her to immediately look away. But she didn't. Her gaze stayed locked with his, and he couldn't help hoping that was a good sign.

At this point, he'd pretty much take anything he could get. He started to cross the room to talk to her, but the song ended, and then Janet, Tammy, and Caitlin gathered around the microphone.

"This year, we have a lot of great awards to give out, so let's get started," Janet said.

Jared didn't care about the awards. He only wanted to make his way through this crowd so he could talk to Leigh. It wasn't easy, especially once they started announcing the winners. Who had traveled the farthest to come to homecoming, who had traveled the least. Yeah. Yeah. He tried to see Leigh, but he could no longer make her out in the crowd.

Why didn't they hurry up and finish these blasted awards?

"And for the most likely to eventually employ all of us, Nathan Barrett," Caitlin announced.

Jared stopped and watched Nathan climb the

steps to accept his award, which was actually a stuffed panther toy.

"Gee, thanks," he said.

Poor guy. Jared really felt for Nathan. But true to form, Nathan was taking it with good humor.

They continued to give out awards, but rather than thinning the crowd, it seemed to actually make the people push closer to the stage. Finally, there was a small break, so he cut through.

And Leigh was standing there, not three feet from him.

"Hi," he said, coming over to her.

"Hi."

For a moment, they just looked at each other. "I'm sorry about—"

"I feel badly about—"

They both laughed.

"You go first," she said.

"Okay. Leigh, I was wrong to push you the way I did. You don't have to fall in love with me, and we certainly don't have to get married. All I'm asking is to be with you and that you don't mind if I'm in love with you."

She was grinning at him. "That's so sweet. But I shouldn't have backed you into a corner, either."

Jared was leaning down to kiss her when he heard

Janet say, "And the award for the person most likely to get arrested, Jared Kendrick."

Ah, hell.

He lifted his head, but before he could say anything, Leigh made a growling sound and stormed the stage. Baffled, he watched her take the stairs in a bound. Then she grabbed the microphone out of Janet's hand and faced the crowd.

"What's wrong with you people? Jared was a kid when he did all those things. You need to let it go and get on with your lives. You can't tell me each and every one of you doesn't have things in your past that the rest of us could rub in your face."

Janet started to take the microphone back, but Leigh glared at her. "Janet, you of all people shouldn't want someone's past thrown in their face."

With a gurgling noise, Janet moved away. Jared's attention shifted back to Leigh. She looked magnificent up there, defending him.

Man, he loved her.

"And for the record, you should thank your lucky stars we had Jared. He made this town interesting. He kept things lively. But that was a long time ago, and by dwelling on it, you're missing out on what a wonderful man he's become. He's kind and generous and..."

Her voice grew soft. He could clearly see tears in

her eyes. Crying? He didn't think Leigh ever cried. But she was now. He watched a tear trail down one cheek. "And Jared is truly, truly the best man I've ever known. The best man I'll ever know. I'm so lucky to have him in my life."

Amazed at what she was saying, especially in front of this crowd, Jared slowly started walking toward the stage. His gaze locked with Leigh's, and she smiled.

"You know, sometimes you don't realize what someone means to you until someone else says something bad about them. I have to thank Janet for her nasty comments. They've made me face what I've felt for a long time but didn't want to admit—I love you, Jared."

A gasp went through the crowd, and Jared felt his heart thump wildly. She'd said she loved him. And in front of a lot of people.

"I love you, too," he told her. "And thanks for standing up for me."

She grinned and came over to the edge of the stage. Kneeling, she leaned over and kissed him. Jared couldn't believe how wonderful, terrific, amazing this woman was.

And he was lucky enough to have her love him. Life didn't get any better than this.

When the kiss ended, Leigh leaned back and whispered, "Marry me?"

Since she still had the microphone in her hands, that whisper echoed around the gym. Jared laughed. "I will if you will."

By now, the crowd was clapping and cheering them on. When Leigh yelled, "Yes" the entire room broke into applause.

After Leigh set the microphone down, Jared reached out and lifted her into his arms.

"I really do love you," she said, caressing the side of his face. "I can't believe how stupid I was not to realize it sooner."

"That's okay. I'm just glad you finally realized." Then he kissed her.

Yeah, life didn't get any better than this.

※

Sometimes life is too good to believe, Leigh Barrett-Kendrick decided as she slipped into the arms of her new husband for their first dance as a married couple.

"Did I tell you yet today that I love you?" Jared tugged her even closer. "That I adore you? That I'm absolutely crazy about you?"

Leigh pretended to think. "Um, well, there was that one time in front of the minister. No, wait. Then all you said was 'I do.' I don't remember anything about you loving, adoring, or being crazy about me."

He chuckled and feathered kisses down the side of her neck. Slowly, the band started to play something completely unrecognizable but romantic all the same. Jared glided her around the dance floor inside the reception hall.

"Then let me rectify that right now. I, Jared Kendrick, do love, adore, and am certifiably crazy about you, Leigh Barrett-Kendrick. I promise to treat you like a goddess—"

Leigh laughed and wrapped her arms around his neck. "Which, of course, I am."

"To me you are," Jared said.

Oh, well, there was no way a woman could let a man say something that romantic without rewarding him, so Leigh kissed him long and deep. She couldn't believe how lucky she was to have this man love her so. Her life was perfect. Absolutely perfect. She had a wonderful man who loved her, and whose rodeo school was finally taking off. She also had a new job teaching math at the high school, and a family who was too precious for words.

Yes, her life was perfect.

And the wedding today had been perfect, too. That, of course, was thanks to the excellent planning she and Jared had done for the past ten months. They'd made all the decisions themselves, and even though she'd never thought it was possible, they'd had no problem reaching compromises whenever they'd had different opinions.

Now, looking back on the wedding, she had to admit that every detail had been flawless. Not a single thing had gone wrong.

Well, not many things anyway. Sure, her brother Trent's dog, Brutus, had taken a big chomp out of the wedding cake. And Chase and Megan's new son, Kyle, had spit up all over Megan's matron-of-honor dress. And Emma, who was about to give birth any day now to a little boy, had started feeling oddly, so no one knew for certain if she'd make it through the reception or not. Then the smell of that spit-up had made Erin, who'd only recently announced she was pregnant and no doubt also was going to have a boy, to have to race off to the ladies' room seconds before the wedding was to start.

But still, the wedding had been perfect for Leigh because she'd been with her crazy, wild, meddlesome family while she'd married the man she positively adored.

If that wasn't perfect, she didn't know what was.

When they finally ended the kiss, Leigh grinned at her new husband and flicked open the top two buttons on his vest. "Got any plans for later this evening?" she teased.

She felt his hands on the back of her dress, and

she knew for a fact he'd slid down the zipper. She'd deliberately bought this dress because it had a zipper on the back.

"I don't know. Let's see, I may take out the trash. Watch a little TV. Why, you have anything special in mind?"

Leigh giggled. "Um, let me think. How about making insane, unpredictable love to your new wife?"

"Sounds like a plan to me." He kissed her again.

While they were kissing, Leigh flicked open another button on his vest. She wasn't going to be the only one standing on this dance floor half-dressed when this song ended.

And speaking of this song, it was so familiar, yet she couldn't place it. Drat. It was driving her crazy.

She tried mentally humming the tune softly but still had no idea.

Where'd she know it from? Unable to think of the title after a couple of seconds, she broke off the kiss and looked at Jared. "What is this song they're playing? I know I know it, but I can't think of what it is."

He grinned. "It's our song, darlin'. Don't tell me you don't remember it."

Their song? They didn't have a song. Did they? Had she forgotten something? "What are you—" Suddenly it hit her, and her mouth dropped open.

She stared at Jared, then started to laugh. "You've got to be kidding me."

Jared twirled her once again to the music, which was kinda difficult considering the band was playing a slow, mushy rendition of the "Hokey Pokey."

"What else would I have them play?"

"What am I going to do with you?" she teased.

"Love me forever?" he suggested.

Leigh smiled. "Sounds like a plan to me."

Dear Reader,

Readers are an author's life blood and the stories couldn't happen without *you*. Thank you so much for reading! If you enjoyed *Handsome Cowboy,* we would so appreciate a review. You have no idea how much it means to us.

If you'd like to keep up with our latest releases, you can sign up for Lori's newsletter @ https://loriwilde.com/sign-up/.

Please turn the page for excerpts of the other four books in this series.

To check out our other books, you can visit us on the web @ www.loriwilde.com and www.lizalvin.com.

EXCERPT: HANDSOME RANCHER

Don't miss the first book in the Handsome Devils series. Order now.

As she studied him, standing near the entrance to the city council room, Megan Kendall couldn't help thinking what a handsome devil Chase Barrett was.

Everyone in the small town of Honey, Texas, thought so as well. With his drop-dead gorgeous looks and his handsome-devil smile, women fell for him like pine trees knocked down by a powerful tornado.

Even Megan couldn't claim to be immune. She and Chase had been good friends for over twenty years, and he still didn't know she was madly in love with him.

Yep, he was a handsome devil all right.

"Picture him naked," Leigh Barrett whispered to Megan.

Stunned, Megan turned to stare at Chase's younger sister. "Excuse me?"

Thankfully, Leigh nodded toward the front of the room instead of in her brother's direction. "The mayor. When you're giving your presentation, if you get nervous, picture him naked."

Megan slipped her glasses down her nose and studied Earl Guthrie, the seventy-three-year-old mayor of Honey. When Earl caught her gaze, he gave Megan a benign, vague smile.

"I don't think so," Megan said to Leigh. "I prefer to think of Earl as fully clothed."

Leigh giggled. "Okay, maybe that wasn't such a hot idea after all. Let me see if I can find someone else for you to think of naked."

"That's not necessary. I'm not nervous." Megan flipped through her index cards.

Her argument was flawless, her plan foolproof. She had nothing to be nervous about. Besides, as the head librarian of the Honey Library, she knew every person in the room. This presentation would be a snap.

But with puppy-like enthusiasm, Leigh had already stood and was looking around. She hadn't spotted her oldest brother yet, but Megan knew it was only a matter of time before she did.

"Leigh, I'm fine," Megan tried, but Leigh finally saw Chase and yelled at him to come over and join them.

Chase made his way through the crowded room. The city council meetings usually drew a big audience, but Megan was happy to see even more people than usual had turned out to listen to her presentation of fundraiser ideas for new playground equipment.

When Chase got even with Megan and Leigh, he leaned across Megan to ruffle his sister's dark hair. Then he dropped into the folding chair next to Megan and winked at her. "Ladies, how are you tonight?"

Megan tried to keep her expression pleasant, but it wasn't easy. Ever since she'd moved back to Honey last year, pretending her feelings for Chase were platonic was proving harder and harder. At six-two, with deep black hair and even deeper blue eyes, he made her heart race and her palms sweat.

"Don't ruffle my hair, bozo." Leigh huffed at Megan's right, smoothing her hair. "I'm in college. I'm too old to have my hair ruffled."

To Megan's left, Chase chuckled. "Squirt, you're never going to be too old for me to ruffle your hair. When you're eighty, I'm going to totter up to you and do it."

"You and what orderly?" Leigh teased. "And just for the record, I like Nathan and Trent much better than I like you."

"Oh, please." Megan rolled her eyes at that one. Leigh loved all of her brothers, but everyone knew Chase was her favorite. When she was home from college, she always stayed with Chase.

"I love you, too, squirt," Chase said, not rising to his sister's taunt. Instead, he nudged Megan. "You okay?"

"I told her to imagine the mayor naked if she got nervous, but she doesn't want to do that," Leigh supplied.

"I can see why not," Chase said. "Earl's not exactly stud-muffin material."

"Oooh, I know what she should do." Leigh practically bounced in her chair. "Megan, if you get nervous, picture Chase naked."

Megan froze and willed herself to stay calm. The absolute last thing she wanted to think about was Chase naked. Okay, maybe she did want to think of him naked, but not right now. Not right before she had to speak in front of a large portion of the entire town.

"I don't think so," Megan muttered, shooting a glare at Leigh.

The younger woman knew how Megan felt about her brother, and this was simply one more not-so-subtle attempt to get the two of them together. In the past few months, Leigh's matchmaking maneuvers had grown more extreme.

"I don't think I'll need to picture anyone naked," Megan stated.

On her other side, Chase offered, "Well, if you get flustered and it will make things easier for you, you go ahead and think of me naked, Megan. Whatever I can do to help."

Megan knew Chase was teasing her, but suddenly she realized how many years she'd wasted waiting for him to take her seriously.

She'd fallen for him when she'd moved to town at eight. Dreamed about him since she'd turned sixteen. And tried like the dickens to forget him when she'd been away at college and then later working at a library in Dallas for five years.

But nothing had helped. Not even seriously dating a man in Dallas had helped. In her soul, Megan believed she and Chase were meant to be together.

If only she could get him to notice her.

"Hey there, Chase," a smooth, feline voice fairly purred over their shoulders. "You're looking yummy. Like an especially luscious dessert, and I positively love dessert."

Oh, great. Megan glanced behind her. Janet Defries. Just what she needed tonight.

Chase smiled at the woman half leaning on his chair. "Hey, Janet. Do you plan on helping Megan with her committee?"

From the look on Janet's face, the only thing she planned on helping herself to was Chase, served on a platter.

She leaned toward Chase, the position no doubt deliberate since a generous amount of cleavage was exposed. "Are you going to help with this committee, Chase? Because if you are, I might be able to pry free a few hours."

Yeah, right. Megan shared a glance with Leigh. They both knew Janet would no more help with the committee than dogs would sing.

"I'd like to help, but it's a busy time on the ranch," Chase said.

"Shame." Janet slipped into the chair directly behind him. "I think you and I should figure out a way to spend some quality time together."

Her message couldn't have been clearer if she'd plastered it on a billboard. Megan hated herself for wanting to know, but she couldn't not look. She turned to see what Chase's reaction was to the woman's blatant come-on.

Mild interest. Megan repressed a sigh. Of course. Janet was exactly the type of woman Chase favored. One with a high-octane body and zero interest in a lasting relationship.

"Maybe we'll figure it out one of these days," Chase said, and Megan felt her temperature climb.

Okay, so she didn't have a drawer at home full of D-cups, but Megan knew she could make Chase happy. She could make him believe in love again.

If the dimwit would give her the chance.

Janet placed one hand on Chase's arm and licked her lips. "Well, you hurry up, else I might decide to go after Nathan or Trent instead. You're not the only handsome fella in your family."

Chase chuckled as he faced forward in his chair once again. "I sure am being threatened with my brothers tonight. But I'd like to point out that neither of them stopped by to lend their support, and I'm sitting here like an angel."

Leigh snorted. "Angel? You? Give me a break. You could make the devil himself blush, Chase Barrett."

Chase's grin was pure male satisfaction. "I do my best."

As Megan knew only too well. She'd watched him beguile a large percentage of the females in this part of Texas. Why couldn't he throw a little of that wickedness her way? Just once, she'd like to show him how combustible they could be together.

But even though she'd been back in Honey for almost a year, the man still treated her like a teenager. She'd just celebrated her twenty-ninth birthday. She wasn't a sheltered virgin with fairy-tale dreams of romance. She was a flesh and blood woman who knew what she wanted out of life.

She wanted Chase.

After a great deal of commotion getting the microphone to the right level, the mayor finally started the meeting. Within a few minutes, it was time for her presentation. Megan stood, adjusting her glasses.

"Remember, picture Chase naked if you get nervous," Leigh whispered but not very softly.

Megan was in the process of scooting past Chase, who had stood to let her by. She froze, standing directly in front of the man who consumed her dreams and starred in her fantasies.

He grinned.

"You know, I think I just may do that," Megan said. "And if he gets nervous, he can picture me naked, too."

ABOUT THE AUTHORS

Liz Alvin

Liz Alvin has loved reading and writing for as long as she can remember. In fact, she majored in literature at college just so she could spend her days reading great stories. When it came to her own stories, she decided to write romances with happy endings because she's a firm believer in love. She's been married to her own hero for over 30 years. They live in Texas near their adult children and are surrounded by rescue dogs and a rescue cat.

Lori Wilde

Lori Wilde is the New York Times, USA Today and Publishers' Weekly bestselling author of 88 works of romantic fiction. She's a three time Romance Writers' of America RITA finalist and has four times been nominated for Romantic Times Readers' Choice Award. She has won numerous other awards as well.

Her books have been translated into 26 languages,

with more than four million copies of her books sold worldwide.

Her breakout novel, *The First Love Cookie Club*, has been optioned for a TV movie.

Lori is a registered nurse with a BSN from Texas Christian University. She holds a certificate in forensics, and is also a certified yoga instructor.

A fifth generation Texan, Lori lives with her husband, Bill, in the Cutting Horse Capital of the World; where they run Epiphany Orchards, a writing/creativity retreat for the care and enrichment of the artistic soul.

ALSO BY LORI WILDE & LIZ ALVIN

Handsome Devil Series:

Handsome Rancher

Handsome Lawman

Handsome Cowboy

ALSO BY Lori Wilde

Texas Rascals Series:

Keegan

Matt

Nick

Kurt

Tucker

Kael

Truman

Brodie

Dan

Rex

Clay

Jonah

55490982R00129

Made in the USA
San Bernardino,
CA